About the author

Ann Veale was born to a Welsh mother and an Italian father and was nurtured in a loving environment together with a brother and two sisters.

She is married to Peter and has two children — a son, David Paul, and a daughter, Helen Claire — and a granddaughter, Yana.

Ann was educated at Glanmor Grammar school, Cardiff University and Swansea University. She played chess for the Welsh Ladies national team, representing Wales at the thirty-third Chess Olympiad in Russia.

Following early retirement from college lecturing, Ann began researching the life of her great grandfather.

JAMES OWEN

Ann Veale

JAMES OWEN

Vanguard Press

VANGUARD PAPERBACK

A CIP catalogue record for this title is
available from the British Library.

ISBN 978 1 784655 46 4

Vanguard Press is an imprint of
Pegasus Elliot MacKenzie Publishers Ltd.
www.pegasuspublishers.com

First Published in 2019

Vanguard Press
Sheraton House Castle Park
Cambridge England

Printed & Bound in Great Britain

To my daughter, Helen Claire, who encouraged
me to carry on when I was ready to give up.

Acknowledgements

Thanks to my brother, Tony, who planted the seed
and nurtured the growth of this book.

CHAPTER 1
1879

The screeching war cry rang through his ears, and with his inner eye he saw, once again, the violent death of young Billy Hopkins. Blood and guts flowed from the boy's body, like a stream of thick, crimson coated sausages.

James was suddenly aroused from his nightmare, to the sound of his cellmates' loud snoring.

The realisation of where he was hit him like a travelling thunderbolt!

'Christ almighty,' he thought. 'I'm in a prison cell, with two psychotic convicts, who would rob me blind or worse. And what do I do? I fall to bloody sleep!'

Looking around at the locked door and barred window, James felt his skin crawl. Was this how his life would end, swinging from the hangman's noose? "So I have killed, but only when I had to. God alone knows, I'm not proud that so many men died by my hand," he muttered. "But was I meant to hang for the murder of a bloody rat? Has my life been planned out from the day I was born?"

CHAPTER 2
1851

On the tenth of December eighteen hundred and fifty one, David Owen had, for no apparent reason, awaken earlier than usual. He immediately looked toward his wife who was lying beside him in the big old four poster bed. Although she was still asleep she tossed and turned restlessly, deranging the thick patchwork quilt. It was freezing cold in their little thatched cottage, so he pulled back the quilt over her shoulders. Very gently, he stroked her silky brown hair. He was surprised to feel beads of perspiration and tendrils of wet hair around her face. His hand moved slowly down, over her full breasts down to her swollen stomach. She giggled, still half asleep. Suddenly, he felt her entire body stiffen. She opened her eyes and groaned in pain. She took his hand in hers, and held on with a vice like grip for what seemed like an eternity. However, a few minutes later he felt her body begin to relax, and the look of pain slowly left her eyes. "We must be sure," she said thoughtfully, "But I think that was our babe, telling me he's been cooped up long enough. Fetch in the sand timer David. Nia the midwife, told me I must be sure and judge the pains properly, so that I do not call her too soon

As David hurriedly dressed, he made a determined effort to stay calm. He spoke to her with a controlled voice saying, "I'll fetch the timer, but then I'm going to get your aunt Martha, she'll tell me when to fetch old Nia. No arguments now, Martha knows as much about birthing as anyone. God knows she ought to. She's had six of her own and helped half the village women who were afraid of old Nia — even now that she calls herself the Village Midwife, which is just a posh name."

David continued to move hastily as he spoke. He pulled on his trousers and woolly jumper. They had lain on top of the linen box, at the end of the bed. Then he made a dash towards the sand timer, which was kept on the dresser in the living room. Armed with the timer David hurried back to the bedroom. He found his wife standing at the end of the bed opening the top of the linen chest.

"What the hell are you doing now girl?" he asked.

"I've kept my wedding nightdress nice to put on after our son is born," she replied smiling at him. "I want to spread it over the chair to get the creases out. I suppose I should heat the flat iron and give it a rub over."

"Bloody hell," he muttered. "I'll never understand women if I live to be a hundred."

Without further ado he caught her up in his strong arms and carried her back to bed. "I won't pretend to know much about these happenings, but something tells me you're behaving a bit daft, Anne love. So no more fretting about nightdresses and stop talking about our son. It could be a girl and she will be very welcome. Now, please to stay put 'til I get back."

"Don't worry about us dear, you go for Martha," she said with a smile. "But don't fluster and hurry her too much, it's not long since daybreak. I think I'll get some sleep now. I feel so tired, and the babe has decided to give me a bit of peace and quiet." Her voice faded with the last few words and she stroked her swollen stomach as she closed her eyes.

The beaten earth path which led from their cottage down the hill, was covered with early morning dew, which hindered David's progress. Slithering and sliding, he continued to negotiate the fastest route as if the devil were at his heels. When he arrived all was silent. He ran up to the cottage calling Martha's name. Before he got as far as the front door, Will, Martha's husband, looked out of the window shouting, "Who's that? What's going on?" Inside the room his wife was getting out of bed saying to him, "Shut up your noise man, before you wake the children. That'll be young David Owen come to get me for **Anne**. Her time must have come and it's too soon so I'd best hurry. Go and see to him and tell him to keep the noise down, I'll be as quick as I can." Doing as he was bid Martha's husband greeted David with a fatherly welcome and some good advice. "Come and sit yourself down a minute boy. Martha won't be long and you'll need to calm down a bit now." Normally he was a man of few words, but for David's sake Will decided he had better make an effort at conversation.

"What do you think then, David, of the bed loft I made for the kids?" he asked, pointing to the wooden ceiling, which began half way along the room.

"Oh yes, you've done a good job there Will," replied David, trying his best to sound interested. "Must have been hard graft for you, specially getting those thick wood beams wedged between the stone walls and the thatch roof."

"Yes, it was and all, our John did a bit of fetching, lifting and holding for me, strong boy he is, though he might not look it," said Will, with more than a little pride. "You will be thinking along

15

the same lines one of these days, David, building a bed loft, now that you're starting a family."

"Before Martha comes back, something is bothering me, Will," said David, frowning.

"What's up with you then, boy?" asked Will.

"I was talking to old Dewi yesterday. As you know, he was a ship's captain and a very clever man. Well, he mentioned the frightening infant mortality rate." David replied. "Did he mean we would likely lose the baby? I know there have been babies born dead, in the village, and even some mothers that died on birthing."

"Take no notice of him, David. He's gone soft in the head, forever spreading doom and gloom. You Anne is young and…" Will stopped abruptly as Martha came out of the bedroom, tying a string belt around the waist of her thick coat.

"Come on then, David, let us both go and see to Anne. Don't you fret now, the first baby is always slow so we have plenty of time." She looked at her husband, saying, "There's no telling how long I'll be, so you see to the kids and get a fire started. There is plenty of stew left in the pot, so you lot needn't starve until I get home." Martha spoke rapidly, all the while she was moving towards the door as fast as her short, fat legs would carry her. Her amply bosom swayed in opposition to her generous beam, while she moved to take hold of David's proffered arm. David was relieved to know that Martha was at his side and he was on his way home.

By the time they reached the path David was beginning to fight back growing feelings of agitation, at their slow progress. Sensing his impatience, Martha offered him a way out. "Did you light the fire before you left, David?" she asked.

"No," he replied. "I thought I'd better get you first. She is in bed nice and warm mind you, and she promised she'd stay there until we get back."

Martha released his arm saying, "You'd better go on ahead then and light that fire. We are going to need plenty of hot boiling water and a warm house. Go on now, I'll be all right. I've walked these hills, girl and woman, for forty years and more. So, who should know them better than me?"

Without hesitation, David nodded in agreement and hurried home to his wife.

Meanwhile, after a few minutes respite Anne began to feel restless and could not go back to sleep. She rose and wrapped her shawl around her shoulders. As she walked into her living room Anne looked around and felt a familiar surge of pride, and then a twinge of annoyance. Her furniture, particularly the beautiful Welsh dresser that her twin brothers had made for them, shone, but through a thin film of dust. "Regular spit and polish and plenty of elbow grease, keeps you nice," She murmured to herself. "I wouldn't like anyone to see you now." She wanted to dust the dresser then, but she realized that her efforts would be wasted. It would be covered with dust again after the grate was cleaned. The cottage, built of stone and covered with a thick thatched roof, housed but one large room. The bedroom, a set up occupied one corner of the room, beside the fireplace. This was the only area of the room which was made private, by a dividing wall made of mud bricks on one side, and a curtain draped over the other. Except for the dresser, none of the furniture was new. It had been given to the young couple by family, friends and neighbours when they were married. There were the two arm chairs from Anne's mother, and the big, old chaise longue from Aunt Theodora. From David's boss, the Farmer Williams, came the chest of drawers, the kitchen table and two kitchen chairs. The kind Mrs Williams had also 'sorted out' several bits and pieces. Anne and David had gratefully accepted everything they were given, knowing that they were much more fortunate than their peers. Most young couples of their class began married life in lodgings, or living 'through and through' with their parents.

When David arrived back at the cottage, all was quiet. He looked in on Anne, who was pacing to and fro. She had one hand on her stomach and the other supporting her back.

"Shouldn't you be in bed, love?" he asked.

"Not for a minute, David, I feel worse lying down. Where's Martha, can't she come?" asked his wife.

"Oh, yes, she is following behind me." He replied. "She sent me on ahead to light the fire, which I'd better get on with. That's if you don't need me for anything?"

"I'm fine for the minute," she said. "Try to ignore me, just get on and light the fire."

David made short work of lighting the fire and then he turned to Anne, asking, "The cauldron is half full of stew so what will I boil the water with? Martha said we will need plenty of boiling water."

"You'll have to use the big pot a couple of times; I'm not going to see two day's dinner go to waste." She spoke with an uncharacteristic harshness. The pains were coming again and she was praying, inwardly, for Martha to hurry. David nodded in agreement not daring to speak for fear of saying the wrong thing.

Anne walked over to the small window and as she looked out she breathed a sigh of relief. "There she is David, I'll see to the door." Even as she spoke she doubled up in pain, before collapsing on to the chair. David dropped the pot, dived for the door and lifted the latch. Leaving Martha to open the door herself he shot back to Anne, who said, "Help me back to bed, love, it will not be long now, I hope." Martha was opening the front door when she saw David helping Anne to bed. She removed her coat, took out a coarse apron from her carpet bag, and put it on. Carrying her bag she followed her niece and nephew. David laid his wife on the bed and was still holding her tightly when Martha spoke. "Leave her to me now David, you go and see to boiling the water." As David left she turned to Anne saying, "All right now my lovely, Martha's here. We'll see this through together, you, me, and Macnabs in there." She patted Anne's stomach as she spoke.

"I'm all right for the minute Martha, funny old thing is, in between the pains everything feels so normal. Is it always like this?" Anne asked.

"Yes, Anne love." Martha replied. "It's God's way of letting you build up strength for the next bout, and then for the big push."

"Phew Martha, there's glad I am you're here." Anne had always been slightly surprised at the obviously happy marriage that Martha and Will had. On the surface they were such opposites. Martha was as short as Will was tall and as fat as he was lean. Not that Will was thin, in fact he had the same 'stamp' as David. Except that Will was even taller, at least an inch, or maybe more. Also Will was so reserved and often seemed shy, while Martha was usually boisterous and 'happy-go-lucky. Martha took her hand, aware that her pains were coming again. "Won't be long now lovely girl, they're very close together. Hold on to me, take deep breaths, and yell as loud as you like."

Thankful for something to do David had walked out to the back yard well and set about filling the large pot with water. All the while he could hear Anne's cries becoming louder and more agonized. He returned, and taking the cauldron from its hook over the fire, he was about to replace it with the large pot of water, when he heard Anne let out an ear piercing scream. This was followed by a great bellow from Martha. "Anne, Anne," she yelled "It's a..." she paused, and David felt his heart thumping, "... BOY!" There was a smacking sound, and then he heard his son's first cry. Later, he could not remember putting the water on to boil. However, he knew he would never forget the feelings that surged through his entire body, when he heard the strong healthy cries of his son. Tremendous relief, was followed by heart-bursting pride. He sank to his knees and thanked God for his blessings.

James could not, even by his doting parents, have been described as a good or contented baby. From the moment he was born he seemed to have an insatiable hunger. At first this hunger manifested itself in the constant desire for food and attention. Later, as he grew older these desires were accompanied by a thirst for knowledge and new experiences. Late one morning, when James was about two months old, Anne was feeling a downhearted. She had fed him and changed his wet clothes for the third time that day and was trying to catch up with her domestic chores. But no sooner had she started sweeping the floor when James began to bellow. She put the sweeping brush down and went into the bedroom where the baby was lying in his crib. She took him into her arms and he was immediately quiet. "There now my darling," she crooned as she walked over to her armchair, then sat cuddling the babe on her lap. "You know your mammy loves you," she said smiling down at the now contented child. "But this is not fair of you young James. You've been fed, washed and put all warm and comfortable. Why won't you lie quiet for a while, in your crib that your Dad made so nice for you?" She was planting a kiss on his forehead when she heard familiar footsteps and a knock at the front door. "Come on in Martha," she called, "the bolt is off." Meg and May entered first, Martha's fourteen-year-old twins, followed closely by their mother.

"Hello, Anne" said the girls in unison.

"Hello girls, there's a nice surprise to see to see you. How are you home from work today, nothing wrong is there?" asked Anne, greeting the two prettiest girls in the village. The tall slim girls had inherited the Flaritys' luxurious red hair and deep blue eyes, from Will's Irish mother. Their milky white skin and perfect teeth were inherited from their grandmother Thomas. When she looked at them she was reminded of her mother who had been a beautiful woman.

"Anne, we just got caught at the top of the hill when this awful old rain came down," said Martha, shaking off her wet coat. "Come on you two, put your things to dry by Anne's roaring warm fire."

"We're home for a whole week, Anne, 'cos the Master and the family have gone down to the Grandfather's funeral in Tenby," said Meg, who habitually spoke for herself and her twin. "They only took Ivy the maid, to see to the two children and big John, drive the coach. So Mrs Jones, the housekeeper, told us and Doris the tweedy, that she didn't need us 'til the day before they get back." Meg paused for breath then continued. "We've been so looking forward to seeing baby James again. My, but he's grown since we saw him at

Christmas time." Anne smiled and gazed from Meg to May, who had stood silently by while her sister spoke. They were physically identical, but Meg had Martha's confidence and drive while May was more reserved, like her father, Will.

"How do you like your work at the Bevan's, May? Treat you all right do they?" Anne asked the quiet girl.

"Yes thank you Anne," she replied shyly. "Mrs. Bevan is very strict about the work being done her way, but she is good to us under the stairs. She gave me and Meg a big meat pie to bring home, and Mama cut some of it for you and David. I have it here in the bag — look."

"Well now," Anne replied. "That looks a sight for sore eyes and no mistake. Me and David will enjoy tucking in to that. Will you put it on the slab in the kitchen over there, please love?"

Martha looked from Anne to her baby son. "And how is Martha's' handsome boy today then?" she asked, bending over to peek at James.

"I'm at my wits end with this baby, Martha," Anne told her aunt. "I've got plenty of breast milk, but something must be wrong with it. He's waking every hour or so all through the night, not that I care mind you, 'cos he's thriving so well. But poor David has to get up so early and he works so hard. He's desperately in need of a proper night's sleep.

And in the day time if I'm not feeding James, I'm nursing him. I've even got him in my arms while I'm making the dinner."

"Give him here to me a minute, Anne," said Martha holding out her arms to take the baby, on to her knee. "Not much wrong with you, is there boy? If I was you, I'd start him on a bit of gruel before bed at night."

"Gruel already?" asked Anne with wide eyes. "But he's only two months old!"

"He's telling you that he is ready for a bit of ballast, hearty boy that he is. And as for all this nursing, well, making a rod for your own back, you are. Crafty little devil, he knows already that he's got you right where he wants you. When he's fed up of laying down, he's only got to bawl out, and his slave will come a running." Martha laughed and held James high shaking him playfully to and fro. When the babe started gurgling with pleasure, Anne joined in the laughter.

"Well, Martha, if you say so, I suppose I am spoiling him." Anne then became solemn, "But, when I think of so many babies who fall ill, and all the infants who die, then I get afraid to take my eyes off him."

There was a moment's silence while Martha looked searchingly at Anne. "Yes, well I know all about that my girl, lost two of my own haven't I?

But they wasn't healthy. This one's like our John was at birth. All heart and lungs, aren't you then Macnabs?" Martha answered her while she looked down at little James. Turning to face Anne she spoke with a wisdom that came from hard-earned experience. "For every infant death there's a reason. Most of the time it's because the mother has neglected herself, during and just after the pregnancy. Poor people like us have a continuous struggle, just to survive. And there's many poor women, worse off than you and me." Martha continued somberly, "Sorry I am for them too, because I know what it's like to have my man out of work and a house full of kids to feed. So you just thank the good lord for what you've got my girl and stop looking for trouble, 'specially when there's none there."

Anne felt ashamed and she took Martha's hand saying, "Martha, forgive me. I don't know how I could have been so thoughtless, talking of such things, when you've suffered so much."

Martha gave Anne's hand a gentle squeeze as she replied, "that's all right lovely, you're tired out and not thinking straight. That's what comes about, do you see? If you think about things sensibly, it's not so often that the first child suffers. But when the rest start coming and money is short, it gets so that a woman has too much to contend with. When that happens it's not her children, or her man that she puts last, it's herself. So my lovely, you take a tip from me now and take care of yourself for their sakes. As I've said, there's not much wrong with little James. Looks the picture of health doesn't he?" Martha paused planting a lip smacking kiss on James' cheek. "At the moment he's like a little doll, but wait 'til he gets a bit older and more demanding. And wait 'til you have a few more babies to tend to. Then he'll have to learn to share your attentions. It will be better if you start teaching him, that sometimes he's just got to wait."

Anne nodded and sighed, " I know you're right, I'll have to do something for David's sake." She began to rise and changing the subject she said, "What about a nice brew up now to take the chill off you three. I'll see to it."

"Indeed you won't," replied Martha, putting one hand on Anne's knee to press her back down. "You two can see to the tea for us — Anne looks worn out," she ordered the twins, with a wave of the hand towards the kitchen area. "And then Anne my girl, you are going to have a nice rest, while me and the twins look after Macnabs here and sort out the chores."

"Oh no, Martha," Anne said with sigh. "You've got more than enough to cope with. I can't let you take mine on too."

"Don't you fret about me, my lovely, things are much easier now," Martha told her with a smile, "The twins are a great help, when they're home that is. And, at only twelve years old, my Lizzie is worth her weight in gold. She may not have got their looks." She paused, holding up a hand to silence Anne, who she knew was about to protest. "No good saying anything other than this. My Lizzie is even plainer than her Mama, God help her. But, you won't find a harder worker or a kinder girl in the entire world. I've left the little ones with her today, knowing she'll keep them happy as the day is long. That's not all either, my house will be as clean as a new pin and the dinner will be ready when I get home. She will just see to it all without having to be asked."

"Oh what grand help she must be to you then, Martha." Anne replied, knowing that any attempt to defend Lizzie's looks was futile.

"My Lizzie is a born wife and mother. I only hope that when the time comes, some nice boy will see beyond her plainness and appreciate her worth." Martha paused and changed her thoughtful expression into a decisive one. "That's enough nattering from me. Off you go and have a short rest on the bed, Anne love," she ordered gently. "If Macnabs starts his nonsense, I'll make him a bit of weak gruel with boiled water. That'll keep him happy a while." Anne simply nodded, smiled gratefully and did as she was bid. Several hours later, Martha stood over the bed, leaned forward and tapped gently on Anne's shoulder. "Anne, love," she whispered. "Time for me to go because it's starting to get dark." Anne sat up, rubbing her eyes and yawning widely.

"Oh my, Martha, I can't remember my head touching the pillow. How long have slept?"

"Not long enough for my liking," Martha replied. "But I should get on my way before it gets too dark, I sent the girls on home a little while ago."

"Yes of course you must go now," Anne replied, as she was walking around her freshly cleaned house. "Oh thanks, Martha, it all looks so nice and I feel like a different person. Well look at himself then?" she said smiling at baby James. He was half lying half sitting on the big chair, propped up by folded clothes. "Has he behaved all right Martha?" Anne asked timidly. "Don't you worry about him girl, hard as nails he is already. Sit yourself down a minute and drink this cup of tea."

As she handed the tea to Anne she started to laugh. "What's happened?" asked Anne beginning to giggle, because Martha's laughter was so infectious.

"Well, first of all he wore Meg out," Martha began. "She walked with him to and fro, then she played with him quietly so as not to wake you, while me and May started the chores. After a while Meg said if she didn't have a break she'd drop." Martha paused while she and Anne giggled together. "So May took him off her," Martha continued. "The rain had stopped so May asked if she could wrap him up and take him for a walk. I thought that some fresh air might do him good, as long as he was kept warm. May put her hat and coat on and picked James up. I wrapped the big shawl around them both, Welsh fashion. She promised not to let him stir into the cold until they were indoors again, so I felt sure you wouldn't mind." Martha stopped and waited for a response from Anne, who had looked a little anxious when she heard that James had been out of doors. When Anne remained quiet Martha decided to continue, "Well now, you haven't heard the half of it yet," she said and she began to giggle again. When her giggles turned to laughter she put both hands on her fat belly as it began to shake.

Anne forgot her earlier concern and once more joined in the merriment. "What happened then Martha?" she asked.

"Wait a minute, I must tell it in the right order," replied Martha, thinking back. "While they were gone, me and Meg finished the chores. Then I put the pie to warm slow and a few potatoes to bake —

they'll go nice with the pie for you and David. Well by this time I started to get a bit concerned, 'cos May was not yet back with the baby. Anyway, soon after here comes May with the baby in her arms. She had walked with him to our house and shown him off down there. Then she walked all the way to the village, calling in half a dozen houses on the way." Martha paused, as if she was unsure of how to continue. "When she was in the Morgans' house, Lettie's little spoiled brat, Jessie, went right up to him and poked her tongue out. Well, May said it was as if he knew exactly what was going on, because up came his little hand and tugged her hair 'til she screamed." Anne gasped and put a hand to her mouth, but said nothing. Martha resumed, "May made a fast exit while Lettie was trying to pacify her brat with all sorts of treats. Better if Lettie had given her a clip round the ear, for poking her foolish tongue out in the first place!"

Martha broke off from her narrative to take a sip of her tea and motioned to Anne to do likewise. "Anyway," Martha continued, "May showed him off round half the village before she started walking back. Every time she stopped for a breather he bawled and as soon as she started again he'd stop bawling."

"When she reached the halfway mark, just before the church, May met the old priest. He told her he had been meaning to call on you, to see the baby, and how you are getting on. He asked her in to show the baby to his wife. Then," Martha gulped, almost choking, but she continued, "While his wife was making them all a brew, the vicar asked May if he could hold the baby. He had little James on his lap and the nice old man was cooing and rocking the baby. When suddenly his face changed to scarlet, he got up with a start and held the baby at arm's length."

"Oh no," said Anne, anticipating what was to follow.

"OH, YES," said Martha hysterically. "JAMES HAD PEED ALL OVER THE NICE MAN ! AND HE WAS STILL PEEING ALL OVER THE MISSES LOVELY MAT."

By this time, both women were laughing uncontrollably, until Anne stopped abruptly and said, " Oh my God, Martha, I'm mortified, I'll never face the good man again."

"Oh Anne," Martha guffawed. "That's exactly how May said she felt. But no need to worry, the man himself and his wife saw the funny side of it. They cleaned up and sent May on her way with those wild flowers for you," she said pointing at a jar, containing a bunch of Welsh poppies on the window sill. "So your boy has sorted out the village brat, peed all over the priest and worn out four women, all in one day. And him still as fresh as a daisy." Martha said, calmer now, but still smiling broadly. "But if he doesn't sleep tonight, then pigs will fly, and they're very unlikely birds. Now Anne, I really must be on my way love."

"Yes, Martha, I know you must. Thanks for today, and please say thank you to the girls for me," said Anne.

"Yes, I will, bach, but no thanks needed. We're family and we've got to look out for each other. There's many a time when your Mama, God rest her soul, helped me out. Best sister in the world she was," Martha replied heaving on her coat.

"Ta ta for now then," said Anne giving Martha a hug and a kiss, as she left.

David arrived home shortly after Martha had left and Anne welcomed him with a big hug. "What have I done to deserve this show of affection, and me still in all my dirt," he said, returning Anne's kiss with interest. Anne ignored his comments saying, "I think it's your turn for a bit of spoiling my man, so get yourself cleaned up and give your son a big hug, while I see to your dinner."

David looked down at James. "Look at you, there then," he said to James, who was still propped up on the big chair. Recognising his father's voice, the baby held his arms up and bawled. David laughed at him saying, "You'll just have to hang on a minute, bach, 'til your Dad gets washed up and then we'll have a little play." David looked at Anne, surprised, she was ignoring the baby and continuing her task. *'Most unusual,'* thought David as he started removing his dirty clothes. *'Him bawling, and her taking no notice at all.'* A short while later, David was eating his dinner in front of the fire when James began to cry in earnest. "All right, my darling," said his mother, bringing him the bowl of gruel. "You must be hungry now." She picked up the child and started to feed him with a small wooden spoon. She and David watched him in amazement as he guzzled the food. When it was all gone, the baby still looked for more. Anne was delighted as she said, "Good boy! Now you can have your mammy's milk and off to bed." David lovingly watched his wife and child. "This is the life," he said. "That was a grand dinner tonight love, so there's him and me well sorted out then."

James drank his fill and fell fast asleep at his mother's breast. She continued nursing him for a few minutes and then took him into the bedroom and tucked him into his little wooden crib. When she returned, she cleared away David's empty plate saying, "Martha came today and told me to start him on a bit of ballast, you know some gruel. It seems to be working too. He looks so contented and he's sleeping fast," Anne said with satisfaction.

"And that's not all either. Come sit by me and put your feet up for a minute, while I tell you all about what happened today."

The events of this day were to become a yardstick for Anne and David in their behaviour towards their son. For almost two years James was the centre of Anne and David's universe, but they resisted the temptation to spoil him.

James was presented with a baby sister, on the fourth of January 1854, who on David's insistence was named Anne after her mother. At first James resented the appearance of this new being, who took his place at his mother's breast. However, little Anne soon began to notice him and make strange gurgling noises, which amused him. When she grew more aware of her surroundings he would play the clown. The more she laughed at his antics the more ridiculous he would act. Later when she began to baby crawl and bump into all sorts of objects, he became protective towards her. He seemed to be constantly moving things out of her path, but more often he would bellow to his mother who was never out of earshot. "Mammy, come and see what she's done now," became a regular cry. She became known as Nan, which was how the two-year-old James pronounced his sister's name. This practice was taken up by others, encouraged by Anne, because she was not over keen on her daughter becoming little Anne. Also, the new title seemed to give the small individual an identity of her own.

James was also to be responsible for further changes, which were not always as welcome. His inquiring mind and abundant energy, regularly led James into mischief, until Anne, in desperation, was persuaded to rearrange her home and habits. She persistently kept James occupied giving him minor tasks and fabricated games to play. David walled off a small area outside the kitchen door so that James and later his little sister, could play out of doors in safety. This sufficed for play intervals and pleased his wife who was, at this time expecting another child. One day, soon after his third birthday, James discovered that he could climb over the wall. He spent almost half a day enjoying the countryside, before his frantic mother, with Nan in tow, found him. Anne had searched back and forth, uphill and down dale, first by one route and then another. She was ready to give in and return to the village to get help, when she came to the brow of Saint Francis Hill. Facing her were the old abbey ruins, surrounded by blackberry bushes and long grass. Her eyes swept automatically over the familiar scene, coming to rest on a large mound of freshly picked blackberries. Then she saw him. He came from behind one of the bushes, both hands laden with blackberries which he proceeded to empty on top of the mound. At first sight of him Anne did not know whether she wanted to laugh or cry. James looked so comical, his face and little legs were almost covered in the purple juice and he was concentrating so hard on the task in hand, that he was oblivious to all around. However, by this time Anne was near to exhaustion both physical and emotional. Her legs were almost caving in because she had carried Nan at intervals, when the child became too tired to walk. Her head ached because she had been consumed with anxiety, imagining that the worst possible dangers were confronting her son.

Suddenly he looked up and saw her. "Mama," he cried out. "Look what this good boy got for you."

She sank down on to the grass and began to laugh hysterically, "Oh James, what am I going to do with you, and how the hell are we going to carry all those blackberries with no basket?" A few minutes later the frivolity of this reaction to James' escapade dawned on her. Nevertheless she decided to leave the scolding until they arrived home.

That night Anne went into early labor and delivered a still born child. This was the first tragedy to strike the young Owens family and both

Anne and David felt heartbroken. James was never to know of the unintentional part he played in his mother's sudden 'illness'. When Anne related the events of the day she told only of generalities, which included walking with her children over the hilly countryside. She waited a few days before she informed David, in a jocular manner, that James could climb over the wall. David promptly built the wall up higher and the play area was made safe once more. Anne soon regained her strength and James' life returned to normality. Although he usually enjoyed visiting his Aunt Martha's house, he had resented having to stay there for two days when his mother was ill. Sleeping in their loft, with Nan, Lizzie and Martha's small children had been great fun, but he missed his mother. And even though Aunt Martha had said, "Good night, sleep tight, watch the bugs don't bite," James had forgotten to keep his head and shoulders underneath the covers. So he had been discovered and bitten mercilessly, by the midges and bugs that fell from the thatch roof above.

James worshiped his mother and he loved his father, but he soon learnt that the two relationships differed. When his eldest son grew past the baby stage, David instinctively started to guide the boy towards manhood. At first, when James was a mischievous two-year-old, David would dutifully take care of him when Anne needed to rest. As time went on, including James in his husbandry chores became a joy to his father, even when the inevitable mishaps occurred. David showed great patience with his son and in return James learned to respect and admire his father. Anne and David's third child eventually came along in 1856. They named him David, after his father. Theodora followed David into the world in 1858, and in 1861 little Martha was born. Less than six months later, Anne discovered she was pregnant once again. James, who was now almost ten years old, had grown into a strong athletic boy. His height belied his age, because he was much taller than other boys of his years and was often believed to be several years older than his peers. In addition to his height advantage and strength, he was also more astute and daring. He became a natural leader amongst his group of friends. There were about eleven boys, between the ages of eight and twelve years old who lived in and around the village. At any one time, at least four of them would be seen together, looking for 'adventures'. They were a motley group, all from poor families whose parents could barely afford to clothe and feed them. Although they were not, in the main, delinquent boys, they constantly found themselves 'in trouble'. Anne would complain to David that she seemed to be the only parent to chastise their son, particularly when David laughed at some of the boyhood pranks which he remembered from his own youth. He frequently found himself telling his wife that the pranks young James and his pals got up to were harmless. He did not want his son to grow up into a weakling, and so he rarely intervened in the disciplining procedures. However, there were a couple of 'bad apples' amongst James' friends and David dutifully warned his boy against each one. James hated disappointing his mother and he was always filled with remorse when she got upset at his naughtiness. But no matter how hard he tried not to, he still seemed get into trouble.

Being poor meant very little to James during his formative years because his family were the same as most and even 'better off' than some. His father did not earn a great deal of money as a farm labourer but his wages sufficed to cover the essentials and also the occasional luxury. During the summer months most of the children who lived in and around the village went barefoot.

Occasionally a child was also seen to be barefoot in the winter, but this was an unusual occurrence even in the poorest families. James was used to being 'shod' annually, although the first months of autumn, invariably saw him wearing boots which were a size or two too large. However, within a month or two, as prophesied by his mother, 'his feet would grow into the boots'.

The year of 1862, was to form an important milestone in James' life. A new and strong influence came into his life that year, when David and Anne took him to the church school and enrolled him as a scholar. The new clergyman, who was to be his tutor, turned out to be the reverse of James' expectations. He had envisaged a short fat jolly man, who would resemble their familiar old Vicar Jones. Admittedly the new man was not very tall, but that was where any similarity ended. While his mother, father and new tutor conversed, James scrutinized the extraordinary looking man. The minister, Thomas Richards, was a very thin man with brown eyes and sparse brown hair which was streaked with grey. His hollow cheeks rested below prominent cheekbones and his forehead sloped back until it reached the crown of his head. His clerical robes hung loosely, as if they had been made for a much larger man. *'Funny that,'* thought James. *'I wouldn't have believed vicars wore hand-me-downs.'* In contrast to his appearance the minister's voice which was deep and richly modulated, seemed to command his undivided attention. James listened intently and although he could not understand some of the minister's long words, he was completely spell bound. When the adults had dealt with the formalities the minister turned to James saying, "So it seems you are to enter the world of academia, young man."

"Where's that then?" James blurted out, wide-eyed with nervous anticipation of the unknown.

"The world of academia is not a specific place, James" the man replied with a shadowy smile. "It is simply, wherever one can find the means, to study the subjects of current interest. At the present time, your most excellent parents have expressed a desire that you learn to read and write, which will become your subjects." His smile grew wider as he continued, "In search of the means which will enable you to study the chosen subjects, they have brought you to me. Putting both factors together we come to the conclusion that this humble church, will, from the morrow, become your world of academia." By this time James was completely mesmerised, even his mother could barely muster a shaky, "Thank you."

David surprised them both, by calmly offering the man his hand in a firm hand shake, which was taken and returned with gusto. David assured the minister that James would arrive promptly the following morning.

CHAPTER 3
1862

His first day at school was agonising for James. He was unable to follow the lessons, and he had never before been required to sit still for such a long period. When it came time to go home the tutor dismissed the other children, but told James to remain. James, who seconds before, had been so relieved to be going home was devastated.

"You appear to be disappointed in your introduction to the life of a scholar James, which is not surprising," said the minister kindly. "Today you were the new boy and as such you were obliged to wait your turn. Your fellow scholars are at differing stages of learning, according to age and time spent on study. However, they have all begun ahead of you, therefore, you must spend some additional time with me. We will stay together after school, at first for short periods and if this does not suffice, the periods will become longer." That day James was tutored for almost an hour, at the end of which his head was reeling. But when he saw the pleased expression on the face of his tutor he felt invigorated

"You have given me hope today, young man and you must continue as you have begun. In point of fact, I am going to make an exception to the rule of never lending. I am going to allow you to take home your slate and chalk stone so that you can practice your letters." His expression changed to become deadly serious as continued. "You must work hard, for at least one hour day at home and never fail to return with your slate and chalk." James proved to be an exceptionally quick learner and within a few short weeks he had caught up with the lower levels of his class. His mother and father were delighted with his progress and gave him every encouragement to practice his letters. Receiving praise from his father and flattery from his mother (who was convinced her son was a genius) was a welcome surprise to James.

Although he still managed the occasional misdemeanor, he began to spend less time at play and more time at study. Praise was a highly motivational factor in James' improved behavior. The more compliments he received the harder he worked. Winter became spring and as the weather improved so did the attendance of children at the church school. James' friendship deepened with two boys who were at the same level of achievement as he, and they began to study together, after school. Anne heartily approved and prepared little treats for the lads when they came to her house. But even when he was due to study at another house, James would head first for his own home. One day, he arrived home to find his father there before him, which was most unusual. David was sitting in his big armchair looking extremely solemn and Anne was crying. When James entered, she hastily brushed away her tears and told him to go and eat his bread and cheese. By his mother's gruff tone of voice and by the way they both looked, James knew there was something very wrong. Doing as he was bid, he looked searchingly at his father.

"Come here to me, James," said David holding his hand out to the boy. "There's something you should know." Anne was about to interrupt when David frowned at her saying, "The boy is old enough to understand and I want him to know from me." He looked from Anne back to James, his face contorted with misery. "There are hard times ahead for us boy, much harder than we've known before, because I was laid off today." He paused and took a deep breath. "With the coming of the railway, trade in general has gone down for everyone in the village. The master, Farmer Williams, kept me 'til the last, 'cos I'm the best worker he's ever had. But with his older sons already putting in a day's work and the two younger boys ready to start, there's just not enough work for us all." While David spoke the expression in his voice had changed from misery to resignation. "There are our five children, soon to be six, your Mama and me, all to be fed clothed and housed. With no wages coming in, I don't know how we are going to manage at all. The way we have been living will change for the worse, it will be hard on you young ones and even more so on your mother."

There followed a few moments of agonised silence, when James suddenly had a terrible thought. Before he could stop his self he blurted out, "Will you be putting me to the Hiring Fair then Dad?"

"No!" Anne responded instantly, her raised voice echoed the repugnance which had accompanied James' question.

"Now calm down the both of you," David said. "I pray to God that I will never see any of my children at one of those bloody slave markets."

In the weeks that followed James saw very little of his father. David would rise early and scour the countryside looking for work. When he returned home, late each night, the children were in bed and asleep. This pattern continued for several months and during this time Anne managed, as she often said, "to keep the wolf from the door." Martha was her staunch support. David's former master and his wife, also helped them generously. From the time David was laid off, every Saturday a parcel would arrive, from the farm. There was always a joint of meat and an assortment of vegetables.

When winter came and there was no money for clothes and shoes, Anne was hard pressed to make provision for the children, particularly for James. Each of the smaller children were given hand-me-downs. For James, she cut and sewed a pair of David's old trousers and a shirt. Boots were impossible to manufacture, so she cut away the toes of his old ones. Thus making room for growth and at least providing cover for the main areas of his feet. James found them uncomfortable and embarrassing to be seen in. However, wear them he did and without complaint, for he knew his mother was doing the best she could for him. The other children at school were oblivious to the change in his appearance, with one exception. Jessie Morgan and James were long term antagonists and she was always eager to upset him. As they were leaving school one day, Jessie made a vindictive remark about his boots. There were two girls at her side, who joined in her scornful laughter. This was too much for James to bear and he retaliated in anger, by tugging her hair. Jessie squealed, and the minister, who had been within hearing distance was dashing towards them. But he was not in time to stop the offence. "Jessie Morgan, you are a spiteful girl and James Owen, I am surprised at you. You will apologise to Jessie, for pulling her hair. And you madam, will apologise to James for your unkind remarks." They both grudgingly, did as they were bid, before Jessie and the others left. James remained because the minister still held on to his shoulder. "James, my boy, I know you are having a most difficult time at home and I have great sympathy for you all. But, you have no excuse for behaving as you did today. I have high hopes for you, James, and I feel sure that you will not disappoint me. One day you will be an educated man and if you continue to grow at such a rate, you will also be a tall, strong man. Why, you are already taller than Jessie Morgan, even though she's much older than you." he frowned slightly as he continued. "With strength and education will come responsibility. You must develop a habit of caring for those who are weak and ignorant. Remember my words James when you next feel the need to punish an offender. A strong man must learn control." While he spoke he watched the boy's humbled countenance. With a desire to press his point and to ensure James fully understood, he added "Brave men don't hit women James, only cowards hit women." This was the first major reprimand James had received from his revered tutor and he was to remember it with deep regret.

David was not aware of the full impact of their reduced circumstances until January of 1863. Anne went into labour and he stayed at home to take care of the children, while once again Martha was called to help Anne. David was confronted with the hard facts of their extreme poverty when he helped ten year old Nan, to dress the little ones. He could hardly bear to put the patched and worn clothing on his babies. Then he saw James in his old trousers and shirt. Gathering all his will-power, David fought down an overwhelming desire to tear the offensive clothing from the boy. Such was his depression, that when Martha informed him of his new baby daughter he could feel no joy. Another mouth to feed he thought guiltily, when a frightening numbness swept over him. This time it took Anne more than a week to regain her strength. Even then she found herself tiring sooner than before. David had been managing the household dutifully, but all the while he seemed to be in a trance. Anne was worried about him, she knew he was coming to the end of his tether. One afternoon, she suggested that he take a walk up to the Williams' farm. "The Williams' have been good to us David, so perhaps you could thank them and visit your pals the same time." David agreed and automatically tidied up his appearance before setting out.

When he arrived at the farm Mr Williams was outside the farmhouse door, removing his boots. "David, man," he called. "Good to see you. Come and join me, I'm just going in for brew."

Mrs Williams was equally pleased to see David and she promptly laid the table, placing large piece of pie and a cup of hot strong tea, in front of each man. She chatted away, asking questions about Anne, the children and the new baby. David had very little opportunity to reply, for Mrs Williams had a habit of answering her own questions. "A new baby daughter then David? Called Margret isn't she? So I've been told. Anne is over it all right? A fine woman you have to be sure, but you're a good man yourself, David, so I'm sure you appreciate each other." David simply nodded intermittently as she continued. "I promised to go down to see our Mary this morning and it's getting late, so I'd best be off and you two men can talk in peace." When the they were alone Farmer Williams opened a cupboard door and took out a bottle saying "You must take a drop of wine with me, David. Have you ever tried elderberry wine?"

"I can't say that I have ever head of wine being made from the elderberries, Sir, so I'm sure that I have never tasted it." David replied.

Five hours and several bottles of wine later, David felt like a new man. He and Mr Williams had conversed as equals and David had gradually grown in confidence until he felt at ease in the company of his boss. Later, as he made his way home, David felt intoxicated and he wished he had not drunk so much wine. His legs felt like jelly and he couldn't manage to walk straight. When he eventually arrived home, Anne was waiting at the cottage door.

"Anne, my lovely girl, I have had the best of times with the master. We had pie and hot tea, then elderberry wine."

From past experience when her father had staggered home under the influence of alcohol, Anne recognised the signs. Therefore, she knew better than to pass comment, at least until he was sober again.

Remembering how downhearted David looked when he left, Anne guessed that Farmer Williams had made an effort to bring cheer to her husband. This, she understood and was grateful to their former master. She just wished that he had not been quite so generous with his means. She helped him to bed and David promptly started to snore.

The following morning, David rose in a foul mood. After so much to drink the night before, he was suffering the effects of a 'hangover'. Anne had awakened their children earlier, Nan and James were the first so that they could help with the little children. They were made to dress and eat their gruel quietly, while Anne breastfed the baby. She settled the contented babe into the crib as David came out of the bedroom.

"Go and see to the animals now, for Mrs Jones," she said quietly, whilst bustling the children out through the back door. "There's plenty of hash in her back yard and watch you don't get mucky now."

When they reached the pigsty, which was about two hundred yards from their cottage, warning bells started to go off in James' head. Something told him to turn back.

He told Nan to carry on with the others and that he would soon catch them up. He hurried back and entered the kitchen just as his mother was placing a mug of tea on the table in front of his father. Anne's hand was shaking and she spilt some of the tea. With one vicious movement, David rose, swept a big hand across the table which sent the tea flying towards his wife. Then, back came his hand, delivering a smack to her head that made her stagger and fall.

James was immediately possessed by an uncontrollable fury and without stopping to think. "No!" he yelled as he lunged towards his father. David spun around to face the boy as James hurled himself up and at his father with clenched fists. Every ounce of strength that the boy possessed went into a rain of punches, which he planted squarely into the big man's stomach. David had to muster all his remaining energy in order to push the boy back, then he stepped aside and sank to his knees. Vile smelling vomit, spewed from his father's mouth, splashing over James' legs and feet. David looked up at his son in anguish, his bloodshot eyes staring in amazement at this furious young aggressor. Anne cried out, "Oh my God! Sweet Jesus, he didn't mean it, David, don't hurt him." David held up a halting hand to quiet her, as James stood his ground, shaking like a leaf but still too angry to back down.

"I did mean it, I did," James shouted and then, quite unpremeditated, he repeated the priest's words, shouting, "Brave men don't hit women, only cowards hit women."

During the stunned silence that followed, the tears that had welled up inside the boy spilled out and he tried to wipe them away with the back of his hands. David was the first to move saying, "All right, boy, all right now, but don't you ever raise your hand to your father again."

James was still shaking and crying as he replied, "Well you mustn't hurt my mother then."

David nodded wearily and said, "We had better go out to the well and clean ourselves up." James looked towards his mother who was now sitting the big chair, holding her rapidly swelling, reddened face. His father bent to pick up the cloth she had dropped, then he dunked it in the bowl of cold water wrung it and handed it to her. She took the cloth and placed it against her face, with tears streaming from her eyes she wove her free hand, signaling them to leave her. They went out to the well and cleaned up in a dazed silence. James washing his legs and feet while his father dunked his head and arms into the big bucket. David then sat on the wall for several minutes with his hands covering his face, before he rose. Putting one hand on James' shoulder, he spoke with agonized remorse.

"Go now, boy and look for the children, I will see to cleaning up the kitchen for your Mama. And James," he added, choked with emotion, "You were a brave man today and I am proud of you. I was wrong, very wrong and such a thing will never happen again."

David returned to find Anne hugging herself, with both arms wrapped around her chest. She was rocking back and forth, causing the chair to tilt, to and fro ominously. Many months of striving to make ends meet, together with the pregnancy, constant worry and self-neglect she had endured, would have been enough to break a weaker woman. Anne had coped with tremendous endurance, until now. The traumatic explosion which had just occurred between her beloved husband, herself and her darling son, was just too much for her to bear. All reserve gone, Anne sobbed and wailed, bringing forth all the pent up emotion which could no longer be suppressed. David rushed to save her from falling, as the chair tilted too far and toppled to the ground. He was in time to cushion her fall, by clutching her with both arms and placing himself underneath her. They both stayed on the floor where they had landed, in close embrace. He held her tightly, as he kissed her tear stained face and spoke words of sorrow for the hurt he had inflicted on her. When her senses began to return, her sobbing subsided. Although she could not stop the flow of tears, she silenced him by returning his kisses. She laid her face on his shoulder and remained in his arms until all her tears were spent.

David eventually released her, insisting that she must go and lay on the bed, "just for a spell," while he made a cold compress for her face. By the time the children returned Anne was resting, while a healthier looking David was putting the finishing touches to a freshly washed kitchen floor. Eighteen-month-old Martha asked for her mammy and as David told her that her mammy was resting, he sat down, lifting her on to his knee. With his free hand he tapped the other knee as a signal to four-year-old Theodora. The little girl promptly joined her sister on their father's lap. David, who was now seven, and ten-year-old Nan looked inquiringly at their father. But James, who desperately wanted to see for himself that his mother was all right, thought rapidly for a few seconds, then asked, "Shall I go and fetch the baby out, Dad? Just in case she disturbs Mammy."

"That's a good idea, James, you do that," replied David seeing through his son's ruse, but understanding the boy's need. "Nan can be the woman of the house and get us all something to eat and drink. Young David, you can do your share by fetching in some water to boil for the tea." James moved slowly into the bedroom and tiptoed past the crib, to take a closer look at his mother. She opened her puffy eyes and saw her son's anxious stare. "Are you all right now, Mama?" he asked in a whisper.

"Yes, my dear," she replied quietly. "I'm just having a bit of rest."

Feeling reassured, he said, "I'll just take the baby out there with us, then you can have a nice sleep, Mama."

Anne smiled at her son and said, "Thank you, James, there's a good boy you are." He clumsily, but securely, took the baby in his arms and left his mother. James sat down, opposite his father nursing the baby, while David quietly told a story to the two small girls. A knock came at the door, just as little David was returning with the water. He gave the water to Nan and opened the door.

"Dad, it's Thomas Williams, from the farm." called young David.

"Call the young man in, David, don't let him stand waiting," said his father.

Thomas, the eldest son of Mr Williams the farmer, entered removing his cap. "Good day, and welcome to you Thomas, come on in and have a seat," said David, smiling at the teenager.

"Good day to you, Mr Owen," Thomas replied, politely, but he appeared embarrassed.

'The poor lad is uncomfortable, about me having been let go,' thought David.

"Dad asked me to come and say, would you be able to give us a hand for a couple of days, starting tomorrow. It's lambing time and we're getting a bit pushed to manage all the work you see," said Thomas. When he saw a smile spread over David's face, the young man relaxed and began to feel much more comfortable in the present company.

"Why now, that sounds all right to me. Just what I need Thomas, to get these lazy bones working again." His three older children and Thomas joined in his laughter, realising that he had made a joke, which also served to lighten a serious situation. Thomas declined Nan's shy offer of a hot drink, saying his mother had his dinner waiting, and he left.

Anne was awakened by the sounds of laughter. She put a hand to the throbbing head, which reminded her of what had happened earlier. She felt all over her face for signs of swelling and found just a little, on the offended cheek. Looking into her mirror she murmured, 'There is no bruising either, so hopefully I will not be asked for explanations.' Anne need not have worried, for when she confronted her family, she was convinced her face must look normal. Except for little Martha, they all spoke at once, each one wanting to be the deliverer of the good news. Theodora had jumped off her father's lap and went to her mother, followed by little Martha. David rose and walked towards his wife saying to the children, "Quiet now all of you. Come and sit down at the table, Anne. Nan prepared food and her brother David helped, while me and James saw to the little ones."

David put his arm around her shoulders and led a perplexed Anne to the table. "Young Thomas Williams has been here to ask me, yes, ask me mind you! Would I do a couple of days work for the master?" David said, trying to sound casual, but he was unable to resist a slight grin of pleasure.

"Well, indeed," said Anne. "That is good news. I can't wait to hear how this came about. I must feed the baby as we talk, I can see she's getting irritable". James placed the baby in her arms and Anne smiled at him saying, "She should be bawling by now because her feed is long overdue. I think she must have been very contented, with her big brother spoiling her." Anne held the baby in one arm and reached out to James with the other. She clasped his hand and looked deep into his eyes. Though her head still throbbed, she managed to smile softly at the boy. In that moment, powerful, choking, waves of pure love, flowed between mother and son.

David rushed home the following evening with his two day's wages (one in advance) and more good news. When he saw that his wife looked no better, his joy was dampened. "How are you feeling today, my love? Is that awful headache no better?" Anne made an effort to smile as she nodded saying,

"I'm all right now, David. How did things go with you then?"

"Well now, Mr Williams is going to give me at least one day's work every week until the end of the season. Then there will be extra work for me when the cattle are taken to Carmarthen," said David. "Even when the cattle go by the new railway, they still have to be herded to Saint Clears and I will either help with the droving, or do young Thomas' work if he droves. But, if I've pegged the Mrs right I guess that she will want to keep young Thomas home, and away from temptation. So I'll probably be droving." David paused wanting to broach the next subject tactfully. "That will be good news, because after the sale, the master will put in a good word with the buyer to take me on. Then if the herd is going to Swansea or further, I could end up with several weeks work, and as you know a drover's pay is much better than what a labourer gets." David hesitated. He had seen Anne's expression change as her pleasure became concern. "I know it will mean my being away from home for a while, love, and that's not much to look forward to, but it's the best I can hope for at present. I won't stop trying for a proper job mind you. and in the meantime, our James is almost as big and strong as most of the men around here. He'll be a great help when I am away on the drove."

During the months that followed David worked as promised two days each week on the farm. The remaining days were spent with James preparing the boy for his future role. David accepted the first offer of droving work with a small measure of relief. Apart from his two day's work at the farm, there were no longer enough chores to keep him occupied. On the day of his departure, Anne and the children walked as far as the end of their path, for their last minute farewells to David. He hugged and kissed each of the little ones telling them to mind their mother and be good children. He hugged young David, saying, "James will need your help, son, to see to the chores. As he helped me now you must help him. Remember now, David, it is no longer play. James must do a man's work and I am relying on you to help him. Don't look so solemn, boy, it won't be for long, I'll be home before you know it."

Young David nodded saying, " I can work hard Dad, but does James have to be the boss?" David looked towards James and then at Anne who could not hide a grin.

"So James has started already, has he David? Well let's put it like this, boy — on the farm as you know Farmer Williams is the boss. When he is away, Thomas, his eldest son is in charge and the younger boy helps his big brother. So you see that is how things work."

"Yes, Dad, but will you tell him no thumping me if I do something wrong then," replied young David with a sigh of resignation.

David turned to James putting a hand on his shoulder "Hear that, son, no fisticuffs between brothers, right?" James nodded and David continued, "You're the man here while I'm gone. I am relying on you, James and I know you won't let me down." He looked around and included everyone in his following statement. "If it happens that I am away longer than expected, I want you all to be pleased not sad. Because it will mean I have got more work and then I will be able to bring home nice surprises for you all."

Nan, who had been standing next to her mother in silence, was looking up to her beloved father with tears in her eyes. "Well, now and what's this I see? My beautiful girl mustn't spoil her lovely face with tears. Come on now, dry your eyes and give your old Dad a big hug." He stooped and taking her into his arms he whispered in her ear, "Hush now my angel, your Dad loves you too much to stay away long. Besides if the babies see you cry, they'll start bawling and we don't want that do we?" Nan managed to return her father's smile.

"No fear Dad, once they start they don't stop," she replied.

"Will you take the baby for me a minute, Nan?" asked Anne giving little Margret to Nan. When Nan had the baby in her arms Anne turned to David, "No more of a to do now, love, just give your wife a kiss before you go, and stop worrying about us." She hugged him closely for a moment as he returned her kiss. "Why anybody would think you were abandoning us, going off to America or far away," Anne continued in an attempt to lighten the situation.

"Well now, that's quite right," David replied gratefully, as he turned to leave. "Ta-ta now then and I'll see you all soon." David finally took his departure with his mind in a whirl. He was excited at the prospect of new challenges ahead and yet there was a surge of guilt, albeit unwarranted, when he wove goodbye to his downhearted family.

During the first few weeks following his father's departure, James found it relatively easy to carry out his deputy duties. His father, with his help, had brought all the heavy chores up to date, leaving only the lighter, daily and weekly maintenance. Therefore James was able to continue with his schooling during the days and in the evenings in and help at home. His extra studies in the early evening were frequently neglected.

However, he was now so far ahead of his peers in his studies, that this was not cause for concern. Also he had for some time been teaching Nan, who constantly sat at his side while he studied. She too was an apt pupil and anxious to please James whom she hero-worshiped. The family had settled into the new routine. Although Anne missed her husband desperately she was amazed at the change in her older children. Nan, who had always been a help to her domestically, continued with added vigour. Nan would rise early each morning, tidy the house and keep little Thea and Martha out of mischief, so that her mother could attend to the needs of baby Margret and prepare breakfast. James would clean out the grate and light a fire using wood he had chopped the evening before. Although the children rallied around for their mother, James saw no harm in reminding them occasionally of the Hiring Fair. Their father, he would say, was away working hard to keep them all from that terrible fate. So if they did not pull their weight, Dad would have to come home and put them out for hire. This speech was usually aimed at young David.

When he returned home six weeks later David was laden with presents. There were sweet treats for all the children and a carpet bag full of good things to eat. A large pork pie, a huge slice of salt beef, a monstrous chicken and plenty of vegetables.

"Oh my goodness me!" said Anne as Nan helped her to unpack the bag. "There's more than enough food here to feed this family like kings, for a month of Sundays."

When young David saw the pie he couldn't avoid blurting out, "Can we have the pork pie for tonight then, Mama?"

"Oh dear," said Anne with mock severity. "I don't know about that." She chuckled and continued, "Well, if your face falls any lower it will touch the floor, so I suppose I'd better prepare a pork pie feast then hadn't I?" The children agreed in unison with a hearty, " YES!"

Anne began to take the pie towards the kitchen, when David took her hand, holding her back. "Oh, but I have not finished with you yet woman of mine — there's my wages." David, grinning from ear to ear, placed small money pouch on the table and held up a paper parcel. "And this, is for the best wife a man ever had," David said handing the parcel to Anne.

The string was tied so tight that Anne's trembling fingers could not untie the knots. "You'll have to help me, cariad, I'm too excited and clumsy," she said, beaming at her husband. David loosened the knots in the string, but made Anne unwrap the paper. She gasped with delight, as she held up the most beautiful Welsh shawl she had ever seen. "Oh David! Oh children look at this, have you ever seen such colours ? Red, brown, oatmeal, yellow. Oh dear me, however did they put so many colours in one shawl," she cried, placing the shawl around her shoulders. "Just wait 'till I show Aunt Martha and the girls. Oh, thank you, David, this is the best present I've ever had." The children laughed, joining Anne as she danced around the room, wrapped in her lovely shawl. David beamed at each of them in turn.

Later that evening, when the children were asleep, David and Anne sat closely together on the big old sofa discussing David's absence. "What did you really think of James teaching Nan to write David? Oh I know you told her how clever she was, but were you just being kind?"

"Not one bit, cariad, why the girl does us proud. She is a marvel with you in the house and, she has got a good head on her," answered David.

Anne smiled at her husband. "Yes, love and so, do you think it would good for her to go to school with James? David looked surprised. "Well, I don't know love, her being a girl like and more use to her Mama at home." He noticed a slight frown appear on Anne's forehead and quickly continued, "But if you can manage without her and it's what you both want, then you'll get no objections from me."

"That settles that then. I want you to tell her tomorrow. She'll be over the moon." Anne clutched his hand smiling into his eyes. "At the same time you can tell young David that if he follows Nan's example he will go to school next year."

David returned her smile and nodded in agreement. He rose and taking her in his arms he said, "The fire is almost dead love, shall we off to bed now?"

James lay on his pallet in the loft listening to the voices of his parents, followed by love making noises. He had known for some time what happened between a man and wife at night. So the strange squeals and groans emitted from his mother and his father, no longer gave him cause for concern. He was so happy that he fought against sleep he wanted this magical night to last and last.

The following week David joined by James took Nan along to the church school for her enrolment. The Reverend Thomas Richards appeared to be unusually excited, greeting them enthusiastically. Beaming at them both, he then hastily bid James to take his sister to the beginners' class and return, post haste, to the vestry. Taking David's arm he guided his guest towards the vestry which was a small room at the back of the alter. When James joined his tutor and his father the cleric was standing at his table, with a newspaper and a letter in his hand. He was addressing David. "This morning I received an invitation to enter a choir in the Swansea Eisteddfod. It will take place one year from now." He paused as he noticed James hovering at the door. "Come along in boy. I want you to hear this," he said, holding up a newspaper. Tactfully, he held it towards James, because he was unsure of David's ability to read. "As you see, written in this copy of 'The Cambrian', the Eisteddfod will be held over two days. The first day will be for solo artists and the second for choirs. The organisation and adjudications will be by self-taught clergy, and two well-known Welsh tenors. The pavilion will cater for over a thousand people. There are expected to be choirs from all over Wales. More than three hundred voices in all — from gentry, colliers, forge and farm workers, factory workers and labourers. There will be no class distinction between the vocalists."

David, finding the good man's enthusiasm catching, smiled back at him saying, "I'm sure this must be a grand thing sir, I am heartily pleased for you."

Thank you kindly, Mr Owen and now I will come to the point in question. That is, a thought occurred to me, when I was digesting the good news." He looked from David to James and then back to David, as if he were going to choose his words with more care. "The point is this. I know that James is a more than passable boy soprano. He would be even better if he attended choir practice more often." James bowed his head, thus avoiding the glare of his tutor's eyes. "I also know Mr Owen, from listening to voices of my congregation during services, that you are a naturally melodious, strong tenor." He hastily continued as David attempted a rebuttal. "It would give me great pleasure to see you both enter the Eisteddfod. There are other people from our parish whom I intend to approach with the same proposition. It is my expert opinion, that the voices of Llanboidy are as rich and sweet as in any other part of Wales.

"Please bear in mind that all your expenses will be met by the Eisteddfod Committee. This includes return train fair to Swansea and also board and lodge with a reputable landlord or lady." He hesitated when he saw a look of concern on David's face. "Whose establishment, I hasten to add, has been inspected by a member of the committee."

"The choirs will sing on the second day, this means we need to allow for three to four days, including the two nights in lodging. As for aid, all manner of financial assistance will be allotted. This will include the choristers' matching attire. I realise you have other most important commitments.

Therefore you will need time think over this proposition."

James had watched and listened with mounting eagerness until he could not contain himself. "Ooh Dad, Swansea, and in a train. Please Dad, say we can go, will you say we can go Dad?"

David sharply stopped his son's pleadings. "Wait a minute boy, calm down and hold your horses. I don't know what to think or say for that matter. Like the good man said this is a big thing for us and it has to have some thought. You had best go back to your lessons, or what it is that you do, and I'll go home and have a talk with your mother. Just you remember, boy, that I have to leave her and the little ones all too often, when I go off working. That can't be helped, but this now is a different kettle of fish altogether. So you leave me to talk with your mama." David rose and put out his hand to Reverend Richards. "Thank you, Reverend Richards, for thinking of us," he said solemnly. "And I must tell you how grateful me and my Anne are, for what you have done for our boy here. Now then, we know our James sings like a bird and glad we are. But as for me, I can settle cattle down with a few quiet verses of Calon Lan and join in with everybody at church, but that's all. Though I am not one to say I know more than you sir. So, if it is your wish that I and the boy go with you to Swansea, I'd best be off home and put it like that to Anne."

When David arrived back at the cottage Anne was in the back garden, showing her sprouting vegetable plants to Aunt Martha and Lizzie. "Hello there," he called.

"Hello, David," they replied.

"Come on then, girls," said Anne. "We can have a brew while David tells us how Nan has settled in school."

David was nonplussed. He silently reprimanded himself for forgetting his dear little Nan, on her first day at school !

As they walked into the kitchen David gathered his thoughts together. "Young Nan will be all right, she is with the lot of early learners. So after what our James has shown her at home, she should fare well."

While they were enjoying their hot drink and baked scones, David decided now was the time to pass on the vicar's offer. They heard a gasp from Lizzie , who was perched on the fender box at the fireside. "Oh my, the Swansea Eisteddfod, just imagine that!" she exclaimed.

As if he were mirroring her thoughts David said abruptly "Yes, yes, I'm sure it will be grand and all that, but, even though most things will be paid for a trip like this is bound to cost money that we can't afford. Besides this, I'm not willing to go off jaunting with James, leaving you and the little ones all the time." He looked steadily at Anne.

Silence followed for several moments until Anne spoke resolutely. "I will not hear of our boy and you David, missing such a wonderful opportunity, and that's that." Her voice softened as she continued, "Now then, I will have to tell you a little secret. I have been putting by some of the extra droving money, David. I managed fine before, on your two days a week, and it's not in me to waste. So now it can be put to good use."

"Oh, Anne, love, I can't let you part with that," said David, who had known all along about the little money pouch in Anne's trinket box. "It's my guess that you have been keeping that bit by, in case the hard times come back."

"Yes, well," Anne replied, "Maybe I have only looked at the black side of things." Her speech faltered but she continued. "Anyway we have a full year and more to go before the Eisteddfod, so you two keep in good voice, then God willing, you shall both go."

During the following year of 1864 Anne became increasingly anxious about her eldest son. Most of James' peer group had long since been put out to work, and she knew that James was still at home 'on borrowed time'. And the dreaded 'Hiring Fair' was overdue at the village!

CHAPTER 4
1864

The answer to Anne's prayers came during the first week of February in 1864. The Reverend Thomas Richards approached James with an unexpected offer!

"James, my boy, I have a proposition to put to you. It concerns the over population of my classes, and the fact that you have reached such an advanced stage in your education. As you know our numbers have swollen, to the extent that I am no longer able to maintain my accustomed high standard of teaching. It follows therefore, that I need an assistant and in my humble opinion, the best person for the post is my star pupil, even though he is barely twelve years old. That is to say, James, with the approval of your good parents, you will tutor the youngest of the church scholars in the art of writing. We will of course arrange a schedule for your attendance at practice for the forthcoming Eisteddfod."

James looked incredulous which caused the cleric to smile. "Furthermore, James," he continued, "As the parish has grown so the church funds have swollen. Enough in fact, to suggest that we can well afford to provide a part-time assistant, with a modest remuneration. Off you go now, James and discuss my proposition with your good parents, you can give me an answer tomorrow."

"Yes, sir," replied the boy. "Thank you sir, oh thank you sir. My father is away on a drove, but I know my mother will say yes, and she will be so glad of some extra money." James ran home, that day with wings on his heels, his mind working as hard as his feet, persistently recalling every word that had been spoken. By the time he arrived at the cottage he was able to relate Reverend Richards's offer, verbatim, to his mother.

Anne listened to her son with mounting pleasure, when he eventually stopped talking, she took his hand and said, "Why James, love, you are right when you say we can do with the extra money, it will come in more than handy. But at this moment, I think more about how well you have done and how proud your father will be when he knows." She stopped and giggled, before finishing with, "What a grand time this mother will have, bragging to all the women by the village well, about my clever boy. Though I suppose I had better get used to calling you a man now, James, for a working man you will be from now on."

James could barely contain his excitement. "Oh, but Mama, I wish Dad was here now, it could be as much as two more weeks before we can ask him." He paused as a horrible thought came into his head. " You don't think he'll say no do you? I mean to say, I won't stop doing my chores here mind you, and you can have all the money I earn."

Anne raised a hand saying, "Stop there, James Owen, you're talking nonsense. I should know your father by now. As I said he will be as proud as punch of his son. And, as for the money, I think we had best think first of getting you something more suitable to wear. A teacher, even if he is only an assistant, is expected to look a cut above the scholars. But we will have to make do until you get your first wage, so the sooner you start earning the better."

On his return to school the following day James told his tutor of Anne's decision. By the beginning of that same afternoon, Master James Owen was introduced to a small group of scholars, ranging in age from six to ten years old. The following weeks passed all too rapidly for James. He was up at the crack of dawn each morning with his younger brother David, ensuring that all their chores were carried out before they and Nan left for the church school. After school James would attend choir practice with some of the other children, who now included young David Owen. Also, the Reverend Thomas Richards held choir practice every Sunday, after service, on the village green. On rainy days, however, practice would be held in church, when most of the congregation would remain after service. Those who were taking part and those who wished to stay and listen.

Great excitement spread through the village as the event drew near. All conversation seemed to centre around the forthcoming Eisteddfod.

When the time came for the choir to leave, every able-bodied person in the village turned out to see them off. Horse-drawn carts and traps were fully loaded with passengers and provisions. Several of the farmers and their sons were on horseback and ready to lead the way to the railway station. Having said their goodbyes, Anne and her remaining children stood alongside Martha, and *her* remaining children. The men who had failed to be selected to sing were accompanying the procession, as far as the station. They were needed to drive back the horses, carts and traps. "Well, now," said Martha, "This is a sight for sore eyes. Have you ever seen anything like it?"

"Never in my life," Anne replied, "And I dare say there is not a person in this village who has either."

"What now then Mama?" asked Meg "After all that, weeks of working, preparing and bustle for the men to go jaunting. We are left here, flat as pancakes."

Martha had no answer for her. But Anne, looked at the downhearted girl and smiled. "I'll tell you what," speaking as she linked arms with the twins. "We'll go back to my house. Mrs Williams sent me down a lovely hock, and I've made a pot of pea and ham soup for us all. We can gossip and be as lazy as you want for the rest of the day. Then we can do what we like 'til the men return."

Lizzie laughed, linked arms with her mother and Nan saying, "Now you are asking for something, Anne. How are we going to get my mother to sit still for five minutes? Never mind the rest of the day."

Anne returned her laughter before calling to the rest of the children. "Come on then you lot, wave to the last of the wagons, then it's time to go home. Thea you take little Margrets hand, and little Martha, can take Aunt Martha's other hand."

David and his sons, James and young David, sat on the floor of an open horse drawn cart. In the same cart sat Will and his son John. Reverend

Thomas Richards sat up front with the driver Geraint. "What's the drovers rest like, Dad?" young David asked his father.

"Well, it's just a big old field where the drovers stop for a rest over. There's grazing for the cattle, a well and a long shelter for the men to bed down," David replied.

"How long before we get there, Dad?" was the boy's next question.

"Not before dark, I should guess, boy, but you will see plenty in the morning," said his father, hoping in vain, to halt the inevitable stream of questions and chatter from the boy.

James and John remained quiet, each enjoying the sights and sounds of the scenery that surrounded them. As they passed through each village the inhabitants would wave to them, cheer, and shout greetings and good luck. The first wagon, driven by farmer Williams, made its way into the drovers rest as night was falling. "We had better get some of these oil lamps lit boys," he shouted to the men in the following wagon. "It will be pitch black before the last of us is in place."

"Shall I take our other lamp over to the shelter, Dad, and sort out a sleeper patch?" called young Thomas Williams to his father as he climbed down to the ground.

"You do that, boy, and take with you the blankets and the basket of food your mother packed," replied his father, who was unhitching a horse.

The remaining wagons followed farmer Williams' example, each driver lighting his oil lamp in order to guide the following wagon into its parking place. More than half the vehicles were in place by the time Geraint drove through the centre of the well-lit pathway in the field. James gazed at the rows of lights in front of the wagons to his left and right before his eyes settled on the shelter. "Wow, Dad," he said. "This is a grand show, and is that where we bed down tonight?"

"Yes, boy, but sit down now and give Geraint a chance to park our wagon tidy," replied David, who then turned to his younger son and said, "Rouse yourself young David, we have arrived and there is much to be done. You can help James with the bedding and the food baskets. The reverend and I will go ahead and sort out sleeping places."

Will spoke to his eldest son. "John, you will help Geraint and me to unhitch the horses."

When at last their chores were done and their sleeping areas made ready, David led his boys to the centre of the field. Everyone gathered around the stone filled dug out, where the farm hands had built a fire. James and even young David were silent as they feasted on baked potatoes, sausages and bread. When the meal was over David said to his boys, "Come on then, you two, get into the barn before you fall asleep out here." Later that night James drifted off to sleep listening to the voices of the men as they sang around the camp fire.

The following morning James awoke to the sound of his father's voice. "Up you get now, James, you must go for a swill to freshen up. Young David has gone down to the pump already with Uncle Will and John."

"What can I smell, Dad? Is that fish being cooked then?" asked James

"Yes, indeed it is. We are in for a treat just now. The fishermen Jones and the Evans boys packed up and brought most of yesterday's catch to share with us."

James ran across the field to the water pump where he joined the queue of boys and waited until it was his turn to wash. John walked up to James and asked him, "You all right then?" When James just nodded in reply, John continued, "Everybody is gabbing away, but you're just stood there all quiet like."

"Well, John," James replied, "I am just trying to take it all in."

"Well, you're not on your own mind," he said, grinning widely. "This is a first for most of us boys here today and perhaps the last, especially for the boy sopranos."

James frowned. "I'm a boy soprano." He paused deep in thought. "But I'm working now as well as my Dad, so maybe we can afford another time."

"That's not what I meant James, don't you know what happens then to boy sopranos when they grow up?" asked John raising his eyebrows.

James shook his head saying, "What do you mean, John?"

The young man took a deep breath before he replied. "Well, James what happens is your voice changes to alto and sometimes lower. Other things happen too, but you better talk to your Dad about that. When happened to me, my Dad and me had a man to man talk. There's nothing to worry about mind you, it's just personal like." He looked around the field as if for inspiration when he spied their fathers. "There's our Dads now waving back for our fish so we had best move it."

"Come on, boys," shouted Will. "Come and have your food." As the two hungry boys ran to their fathers, all thoughts of James' impending manhood were forgotten.

When the fish breakfast had been enjoyed by all, it was time to continue their journey. They reached the train station in good time, arriving just after the local Carmarthenshire Congregation, who greeted their Llanboidy neighbours with warmth. Travelling by train was not as enjoyable as James and the boys from his village had expected. The window areas were already taken by the local boys and men. Soon after, at the following train stop, they were squashed together to make room for the next contingent of choristers. However, when they eventually arrived at the Swansea station the buzz of excited voices lifted their spirits once more.

They left the train and station in much the same way as they had joined it. Local people met them with wagons and carts of all description. David, Will and their sons were taken in a horse-drawn cart, by a Mr Button, a short man of some bulk. He was clean shaven, except for his upper lip, which was covered with whiskers. He introduced himself and informed them that his farm was in Dunvant, west of Swansea town. Will sat up front with farmer Button and David climbed in the back with the boys. During the drive Mr Button chatted in a loud voice so as to be heard by David and the boys who were sitting in the back of the cart. "The Mrs MacIndow, with whom you will be lodging, is a very respectable lady, as are all the families chosen to house the visitors. She is the daughter of farmer Davies, whose very large farm is in Sketty, neighbouring my modest land. Mr MacIndow is a ships' captain and at sea at present. However, she is of the opinion that her two small children and numerous close neighbours would be ample chaperones. In addition to this your highly admired vicar, vouched for your impeccable characters."

They soon arrived at a long row of terraced houses known as Westbury Street. Mrs MacIndow and several other ladies stood chatting on their doorsteps, waiting for the arrival of their visitors. Once the formal introductions were completed farmer Button went on his way leaving the visitors to settle into their temporary abode.

Their landlady looked lovely to James. She had a happy smile, a glint in her dark brown eyes and shiny black hair. She was slim and about his height, well not much taller which made him feel quite grown up.

"Follow me upstairs, to put your things away," said Mrs MacIndow walking ahead as she spoke. "I've put the small back bedroom ready for the three boys and you gentlemen are in the middle bedroom. My children are in the front bedroom with me, while their father is away. Once you have settled, find your way down to the kitchen, where I have prepared food. I would think you are all ready for a bite to eat after your long trip."

"Thank you kindly, Mrs I do hope we are not putting you out too much," replied David.

"Not at all," she said, smiling as she turned to go back down the stairs.

"Hurry up, everybody," said Will, when they were unpacking their belongs. "We mustn't keep the good lady waiting, and I can smell tasty food."

The kitchen housed a large wooden farmhouse table and ten chairs which Mrs MacIndow informed them had been a gift from her farmer father. The Welsh dresser which stood against the back wall reminded James of home, as did the glowing fire in the hearth. Mrs MacIndow's young daughter was standing close to her mother, looking shyly at the strange people walking into her kitchen. "These nice people have come to stay with us for the Eisteddfod, darling," her mother explained, as she helped her little girl on to a dining chair.

Turning to her visitors, she said "Please do sit. This is my daughter Violet. My little son Thomas is at his granny's, and please call me Emma."

"Thank you, Emma and in turn please call me David, and my boys James and young David. William here we call Will and his son John."

Whilst looking around her company Emma smiled and said, "I hope you will all be comfortable here and enjoy your stay in Swansea."

"I'm sure we will, Emma, and thank you again for giving us such a warm welcome," David replied.

"My pleasure. Now, you should all eat your fill and get a good night's sleep. You have a big day tomorrow." Taking her advice they each enjoyed a bowl of chicken and vegetable broth with fresh baked bread, before retiring to their allocated beds.

The following morning James awoke to the excellent aroma of bacon coming up the stairs. John was already dressed, and Will was standing at their door. "Come on you boys," he called to them. "Your dad has gone on downstairs. They were just finishing a hearty breakfast when a knock came at the front door.

Farmer Button had arrived. "Can I come in?" he called, opening the door and walking in regardless. "I came early to leave my wife and daughter to their toiletries. I am nothing for all this primping and preening that the ladies seem to find necessary. I see that you fellows, like me, are already wearing your choristers' outfits. I thought we might spend an hour viewing some of the sights that Swansea has to offer," He suggested, looking at David and Will for approval.

"That's very kind of you sir. What a treat for us and the boys," David replied. "Yes indeed." said Will nodding. " Oh yes please" said James, with

John and young David nodding their heads and beaming.

True to his word Farmer Button introduced the visitors to several local attractions and brought them back, as promised one hour later.

They returned to find Emma filling a basket with packed lunches and fruit. "Have you had a nice time ?" she asked

"Oh, yes," young David blurted out. "We saw the Museum, the maritime quarter and Clyne Castle with battlements and," he paused looking at his father, "What was the building we saw Dad, with the gold stone and fancy columns?"

"The Guildhall, David," his father replied. "Those were Corinthian columns and sash windows that open and close up and down." He turned to Emma saying, "Mr Button also told us many interesting things. He told us that General Wade furnished the battlements of Clyne castle in 1818 and that Graham Vivian recently bought it. Also that the Vivian family were responsible for building the gothic dower house, Parc Wern."

"The Vivian family are indeed a powerful dynasty in Swansea," Emma said. "John Vivian, his son Henry and their partner William Foster own Swansea Coal Corporation and the Morfa Copperworks. However, the largest colliery in Swansea is owned by Charles Henry Smith. He and his wife are friends of my parents. Enough of my chattering now, you will soon be meeting most of these men as they belong to the Swansea choir," she added. She placed a cloth over the food she had packed into the large basket, when David offered to carry it for her.

"Just a minute now," said farmer Button. "I have to go back home and get my wife and daughters. I will be back in less than ten minutes."

Mr Button returned as promised, with his wife and two teenage daughters. The two girls had their mother's looks, both slim and a little taller than Mr Button. The only difference was that they wore their dark blonde hair short and curled, whereas their mother's was severely drawn back into a bun.

"We have just a short walk from here, so I will leave the horse and cart outside if that's all right with you missus," said Mr Button, addressing Emma.

"Certainly, Mr Button," Emma replied. "We are all ready to go. I must say all you gentlemen, and boys look very smart in your choir regalia." She began to walk on with her son and daughter, greeting Mr Button's family. Emma had met Mrs Button a few times, however, they could not be said to know each other well. Emma being much younger, had a different circle of friends.

"Good day to you, Mrs Button and hello girls — you do look very pretty in your Sunday best."

Both girls and their mother said hello in unison. Smiling at Emma the latter replied, "Please to call me Agnes and my husband George. I am aware we don't know each other very well but I'm sure we will after today."

Farmer George Button, David, Will and their boys led the group, with the ladies, girls and little Thomas bringing up the rear.

The streets were getting crowded, and the ladies kept stopping to greet friends and acquaintances, which was beginning to irritate their male companions. " I think it would be best if we chaps went on ahead," George announced to his group, "The choirs have their own entrance at the back of the pavilion, so we will need to split up soon at any rate."

With waves and grins from the females, the men walked on with sighs of relief. More and more men appeared as they got closer to their destination, until the throng became quite an orderly queue. At the gate allotted to the choirs there was a man handing out a programme to each of the contestants. He also directed each of them to the section of the pavilion assigned to their group. Little David took his programme and turned to James raising his eyebrows with a questioning glance. "Don't worry, boy, if there are words you don't understand just ask me or Dad," James told his younger brother, with complete understanding of the boy's dilemma. He was suddenly feeling very nervous and tried to cover this with the big brother act.

"My group is on the other side of the pavilion, boys." said George. "So, I'll see you all later then." David, Will and the boys waved as George walked off, when they heard a voice calling them "David, Will, over here".

"Hello there," replied Will. Being the tallest he was the first to recognize the Llanboidy group. He was able to see over the heads of the people in front of them. "Look boys it's the Evans twins with our lot over here."

James ran swiftly up to the Reverend Thomas Richards "Hello, sir," he shouted, so as to be heard over the din. Everyone seemed to be talking at once, and each with a loud voice.

"Hello, and welcome, James," he replied, in the loudest voice he could muster. "I think we had better wait until the noise abates before we attempt to converse."

The vicar put a hand on James' shoulder and pointed to the bandstand to their right, where the band was tuning up. The bandsmen were all dressed alike, in elegant navy suits bordered with red and gold braid.

A hush fell over the pavilion, as the band began to play, 'Mae Hen wlad fy Nhadau', the Welsh national anthem, and the voices rose. Singing with, and listening to, all these people, singing, with such gusto and passion, sent thrills running through James' body. He was flushed with excitement until the last chord was struck. The first choir waited for the applause to die down before they made their way to the stage. They sang a Welsh ballad which was unknown to James, however, he listened and applauded heartily with the audience. When their performance came to an end, they returned to the centre of the pavilion. This large cordoned off area was designated for the choirs.

Once again silence fell over the audience as the second choir began to sing.

Six choirs sang before the midday break. Each one was met with deafening applause. "Well, well, excellent entries so far," said the Reverend Thomas Richards when they had finished clapping and cheering the final entry of the morning. "What do you think of our chances now, sir?" asked David, looking dejectedly at the cleric. "Llanboidy voices can compete with the best David," the cleric replied, "And I am confident that our choir will do well. Come now cheer up and we will enjoy our picnic lunches that the good ladies have prepared. We are first to sing this afternoon, so make sure you leave some of your water for later, because throats sometimes become dry." As he spoke the cleric looked anxiously at young James, who seemed to be deep in thought. "Anything bothering you, boy?" he asked, holding James back from the group. "Well, it's something John told me, about growing up and having my voice changed somehow. He told me to talk to my father but I haven't had chance yet," James answered.

"Ah, I see," said the cleric. "Very remiss of we adults not to have thought of this. No time for discussion now. Suffice to say, if, during your solo you feel a frog in your throat, close your mouth and nod to me. I will be watching you as I conduct the choir, and subsequently take over from you if necessary. Now we must make haste and join the others."

The Llanboidy choir took their places on the stage immediately after the lunch break, and once again the audience broke into loud applause. The applause died down as the choir began to sing, but, clapping and cheering began again as the audience recognised the strains of 'Calon Lan' an all-time favorite ballad of the Welsh people. James sang with gusto, nerves forgotten, or at least held in check until the time came for his solo chorus piece.

James stepped forward, nodded and smiled timidly at the reverend. His young voice rang out with perfect pitch and articulation, and he completed his solo to tumultuous applause. He stepped back to his place next to his brother with a huge sigh of relief, amazed that all these people were clapping for him. When he returned to sing with the choir his throat felt dry and his voice was hoarse, so he drank a sip of his water. But his voice had broken! Realising what was happening to him James remained silent until the end of their performance.

The vicar told him later, that God in his goodness, had allowed James to complete his boyhood chorus before making him a man.

Two more choirs followed Llanboidy choir and they were able to relax, watch and listen to with pleasure. The last one was the Dunvant Male Voice Choir, 'the local boys' who naturally had the loudest and longest ovation. Then came the speeches. The longest and most tedious, (in James' opinion) was spoken by the Mayor of Swansea. However, all agreed that this had been a wonderful day, a day to remember forever. All too soon the celebrations were over and it was time for everyone to return to his respective lodgings for the night.

Back at Westbury Street Emma had supper ready for her guests — cold roast pork and boiled potatoes. They ate ravenously and talked excitedly of the excellent Eisteddfod day. Emma drew proceedings to a halt when she noticed young David was trying not to fall asleep. "I think it is time now to get your rest — another long day of travel awaits you all tomorrow."

James awoke the following morning feeling strangely sad. He had, for some time had something exciting to look forward to, but now the great adventure was over. He was about to leave the exciting bustle of Swansea and the beautiful Emma. "Come on, boys," David called to his sons. "Breakfast is ready."

"Stop your daydreaming, James," said young David, dressing with haste. "Hurry up or Dad will be mad with us."

James complied and was ready in next to no time. They had eaten their breakfast when farmer Button arrived, as promised, at nine-thirty. "Good morning to you all, and a fine day once again for travelling," he said. "Let me help with the baggage, Will." Emma and her two children said goodbye to each of their visitors with a kiss on each cheek and a hand shake. David and Will thanked Emma for her excellent welcome and hospitality. The three boys followed their fathers' example, thanking their kind landlady.

When the horse and cart began to move James looked back. Emma was waving goodbye. She seemed to be looking just at him, with her beautiful eyes, as he waved back.

During their journey home James was deep in thought, becoming a man had, seemingly, been suddenly foisted upon him. He barely remembered greeting the others, or even the train journey home. He kept thinking of the lovely Emma.

Talk of the recent events and differing experiences kept everyone occupied most of the way home. David, however, was very much aware of how subdued his eldest son seemed to be. The Reverend Thomas Richards had informed David of his conversation with James, concerning the onset of manhood. David agreed with the vicar that James should have been spoken to on the subject before they left home. With this in mind David resolved to have a talk with James, as soon as possible.

When they arrived home Anne and the little girls bombarded them with questions, about what they did and saw in Swansea, how the choir got on, and more. David 'put his foot down' and refused to answer any questions until they had washed and eaten.

Anne had entered the happiest of times for herself and her young family. Her eldest son proved to be an excellent assistant to the Reverend Thomas Richards. Within a year James was taking five classes each week. Her husband, David had been given droving work with a distant cousin of Anne's father, Mr John Thomas, who had built a small farm into one of the largest farms in the county. Because the droving was only as far as the railway, David was given a full-time job as a farm labourer with extra pay for the droves. The Thomas Farm comprised almost twenty hectares, divided into cattle grazing, agricultural and domestic produce. Anne was content in the knowledge that on such a big farm there must always be plenty of work, also David was working for 'family' and this had to be extra security.

Nan was returning with an errand from the Thomas farm, one afternoon when she saw the pony and trap of Mrs Bethan Richards, driven by Joseph Price. Joseph had been a scholar, alongside James at the church school, and was known to Nan's family.

Nan was surprised when Mrs Richards made Joseph stop. She was even more surprised when the wealthy widow told Nan that there was an opening for a bright girl, in her kitchen. Joseph Price had told his employer about young Nan Owen, Who was the sister of his friend James, stressing that she was from a very respectable, hard-working, family.

Anne had extremely mixed feelings when parting with her eldest daughter. Nan had matured beyond her eleven years and was her mother's 'right hand', her friend and her confident. But, she would see her daughter every other Saturday and Nan was going into the service of a good woman. Joseph had told them, 'The widow woman was no one's fool, but if you pulled your weight she was more than fair with you. Nan should get along just fine.'

The following year, David Owen was told that Mr John Thomas needed an extra hand. David was, at that time, harrowing, preparing one of the agricultural fields, for planting. The thick, wooden harrow with a yolk, was pulled by a large carthorse. This work needed strength and control, so the master suggested that David could do with a boy to help him. Naturally David suggested his son, who was a strong healthy ten year old. Mr. Thomas agreed and David's son was hired. Young David was so thrilled and Anne thought her cup of happiness would overflow. Her three eldest children were all working, and the dreaded Hiring Fair never mentioned.

James was approaching his sixteenth birthday, when he decided that it was time to leave home, and make his own way in life. The memories of his short visit to Swansea, and the beautiful Emma had never left him. However, with the passing of each year there had been reasonable cause for his decisions to stay at home. At last he felt that his family no longer needed him — his father David was earning good wages, and for their respective ages so were his sister Nan, and his brother David. This meant his mama would be able to manage without his money. He had been told of job vacancies in the New Dock, Swansea, by his cousin Edward who was of the opinion that James would be taken on straightaway. This being so he would soon be able to send money home to his mother, for the 'extras' that his present wage provided. His problem was, how to tell his parents. He was sure his father would understand, and for this reason he decided to broach the subject with David first.

That evening James hurried from the church to catch him as he was leaving his work. David was surprised to see his son waiting at the gates to the farm, "Anything wrong James?" David asked.

"No nothing wrong, Dad, I just wanted a word with you in private like," James said shaking his head.

"Let us start for home then and we can talk on the way. I'm hungry and your mother will have our dinner ready," his father replied.

During their walk James discussed his plans with his father. David, after some persuasion, agreed to support James when he told his mother.

Little Margret and Thea met them as they approached the cottage. Thea ran to her father, and Margret held her arms out to James saying, "Piggy back, James." James laughed as he hauled the child onto his back.

"You're late," said Margret, frowning at her brother.

"Well, I'm here now, so let me and Dad go in and have our dinner," James replied as they walked into the house.

"The two of you together?" Anne asked looking surprised.

"James met me from work," David replied. "Before we go into the whys and wherefores, I would like to eat my dinner in peace please.

"Not another word was spoken until dinner was over and the table was cleared.

David looked seriously at James and nodded saying, "Time now to talk to your mother." James took his mother's hand guiding her to the big settle where they sat as he unfolded his plans. Anne was surprisingly subdued. "I've always known this day would come," she said quietly, looking at her first born with sadness in her eyes. "As birds fly the nest so do children grow up and leave home."

"It's only Swansea, Mama. It's not as if I'm going to sea, or to America, like some of the boys," James explained. He felt enormously relieved that his mother took his news well.

Anne suggested that James should go into Swansea, stay for a few days, and see Edward, and make sure of the job before burning his bridges at home. This suggestion was endorsed by David and agreed upon by James.

As planned James arranged two days off from his teaching, and took the train to meet Edward, a day before the pre-arranged interview at the New Dock, Swansea. At nineteen years of age Edward was regarded by James as a 'working man' of some consequence, and therefore James was delighted by his cousin's regard. Edward was waiting at the station when James arrived, and from there he took James to his lodgings. On arrival at the house the landlord bid James welcome, and offered them both a hot drink before bed. The boys thanked him and took their drinks up to Edward's room, where they went over arrangements for the following day. A loud hooting noise caused James to wake up with a start the following morning. James sat up in his bed and looked to the bed opposite, where Edward, grinning at him, rose and said, "You'll get used to that soon enough, cousin. It comes from the factory every morning to make sure the workers are on time." They dressed and breakfasted hurriedly. Edward did not want James to be late for his interview.

When they arrived at the New Dock they made their way into the first building. Edward accompanied James as far as the small room used as an office/store room, which was housed near the entrance. "I'll see you later, James, after I finish work. Just knock the door and he will call you in. Good luck," said Edward as he went on his way. James' knock on the door was answered by a loud voice, "Come on in."

On entering the office James' immediate thought was *'What a mess'*. The floor was littered with piles of boxes and canvas sacks, and a waste basket which was overflowing with papers. Mr Harold Morris sat behind a large oak desk. He looked up, and James was confronted by a questioning stare.

"Good morning, sir. I'm James Owen come for the interview," he said.

Mr Morris stroked his grey beard, and said with a nod, "Move that lot over here." He pointed to a chair, with stacks of files. "And sit yourself down." His pale brown eyes, beneath bushy eyebrows, looked at the boy from top to toe. "Well now, James Owen, you look like a strong lad. Think you can handle dock labour, loading and unloading cargo ships? Because that's what the job involves, hard work for good pay."

"Yes, sir, Mr Morris," James replied. "If you give me the chance, I won't let you down."

That was as far as the interview went. Mr Morris was impressed with James' appearance and enthusiasm. James was told that, as long as he was prepared to work hard and do as he was bid, the job was his. And he could start straight away. Mr Morris suggested that the coming Monday would be good. James suddenly looked confused.

"Do you have a problem with something I've said, young man?" asked Mr. Morris.

"No, not at all, sir. But my cousin, Edward, who works for you, brought all this about for me. So I should let him know I got the job and thank him very much. But if I am to get the two o'clock train home today instead of tomorrow, I will miss him." James answered. "But I am so sorry, I should not be bothering you like this."

Mr Morris smiled and replied, "No problem there lad, I know young Edward. He is good worker. I will speak to him on your behalf, and I'm sure he will understand your situation."

James thanked Mr Morris, left the office and made haste back to Edward's lodgings . He took very little time to collect his few belongings before setting out on his way home.

Once on the train James found it difficult to sit still, and with no one to talk to the journey seemed endless.

Arriving unexpected, he made his way through the station alone, acknowledging the station master and greeting a few acquaintances on his way through the village. Anne was at home with the three youngest girls when James arrived. Little Margret ran to him and he caught her up in a bear hug.

'Of all the children, it's this one I will miss the most,' he thought, *'and I fear she will miss me too.'*

"Oh gosh, James," Anne said bustling. "I was not expecting you today. But what am I thinking, fussing about, instead of telling my handsome boy how glad I am to see him, home safe and sound."

James grinned and gave his mother a hug." You all right Mama?" he asked.

"Certainly I am, son," she replied. Then she turned and called to her daughter. "Thea, come and give me a hand. You can get a brew going for James while I prepare the food for him, and your Dad coming home soon."

Later that evening when the girls were tucked into bed, the opportunity arose for James to speak to his parents. They were not surprised when James told them he had been given the job. Both David and Anne were proud of their son. Thoughts of him being unsuccessful had not occurred to them. As they listened to James, David, injected a few questions regarding the boss, and working conditions. Anne, however refrained from comment until her son, looking at her, became quiet. He was waiting, hoping for her acceptance, if not approval. All her well-rehearsed 'motherly' advice, concerning his well-being were forgotten. She simply implored him to come home, if things didn't work out, or if he was unhappy, warning him, of misplaced manly pride. And so the die was cast. James would leave on Sunday and lodge with Edward until he found suitable lodgings of his own.

The following morning James rose early. After a hasty breakfast he set off to the church, intending to approach the vicar before the pupils arrived. The reverend gentleman was preparing the schoolroom when he heard James arrive. He looked up and smiled "Good morning to you, James," he said. "You are early today."

"Yes, sir," said James. "I wanted to have a word with you before the pupils arrive."

"Please don't look so grave young man, I feel sure you have much to be pleased about," said the vicar. "Well, now you did get the job, didn't you?"

"Yes, sir, I did," James replied. "But they want me to start this Monday."

"So be it, James boy. We will just have to do without you a little sooner than expected." The vicar smiled again, held out his hand and patted James on the shoulder. "But don't forget us, you come and see us on your visits home."

"I will, sir," James replied. "How could I forget you, when you have done so much for me. I will always be grateful, and I can't find the right words to thank you enough."

The children began to arrive which brought an end to their privacy, and conversation. School day began and James was obliged to revert to his tutor role. James worked diligently with the children until Friday evening, when it was time to say goodbye. Reverend Richards walked into his class just as James was about to dismiss his pupils. "One moment of your time is required, Master Owen. Hywel Jones has something to say on behalf of your class. Come along now, Hywel, no time to be backward."

"We are all sorry that you are leaving sir," said Hywel in a loud voice. "But we hope you will be happy in Swansea. And we want you to have this to remember us." Hywel handed James a small parcel and quickly returned to his seat, greatly relieved that he had remembered his speech.

James opened the parcel and took out a woolen cap. "Well I never, this is just great. You must have known how cold it is in Swansea first thing in the mornings." He felt quite emotional as he spoke. "I thank you every one, and I must say it has been just grand, working with such clever scholars."

Each child said goodbye to James before he or she left the classroom. When the last one had left Mr Richards held out his hand to James, who shook it saying, "Goodbye, sir, and thank you again for everything."

On Friday evening David, Will and several of the men from the village had arranged a 'send-off' for James, at the local village tavern. They also invited a few of the older boys who were friends of James. A capital evening was enjoyed by all.

Saturday began with visits from well-wishers, relatives and friends. In the evening Will and Martha arrived with their children. Will had brought some of his home brewed Welsh mead and Martha weighed in with freshly baked Welsh cakes and scones.

"Gosh, Aunt Martha, I can't believe all the fuss I'm having from you all," James said. "People have been coming all day and now all of your family are here."

"That goes to show how much you and your family are admired and respected, boy," Martha replied. "It has been quite a while since the last send off, so you would have been too young to take part. Most of the village people, like you and your Mama and Dad were born and bred in Llanboidy. Close community we are, we look out for each other through the bad times, and celebrate together in the good times." Martha continued without a pause, "My Lizzie would have come but her Dewy is away on a drove. With the a baby on the way she couldn't face the trek from the other end of the village."

After a pleasant evening, Will, Martha and their family left at a reasonable hour on account of the children being tired.

Sunday came around all too soon for Anne — her eldest boy was now a man, and she had to let him go. After a night of disturbed sleep Anne rose to the sound of a door closing. She was making her way to the kitchen when she saw a note on the dresser.

Dear Mama, Dad and all,
I decided to take the early train. I will see you all soon as I can.
Your loving son and brother,
James.

CHAPTER 5
1874

During his years in Swansea, James, as promised, worked hard in the docks, and returned home at regular intervals. In 1874, Mr Harold Morris retired and recommend Edward as his successor. But this recommendation was rejected, on the grounds that the position had been offered to a nephew of one of the directors. James was surprised when he approached Edward, to find his cousin had little need of sympathy. Quite the reverse — he told James he was planning a change of job, and would advised James to follow suit. "You know there's an outbreak of cholera on the New Dock cousin," said Edward "I'm concerned about some of the Irishmen working with us — two of them are off work with the disease. And I heard it is spreading among the Irish immigrants, men women and children."

"I know," said James sadly. "The poor devils who fled from Ireland because of the potato famine, are packed into poor housing in Greenhill —

dozens of families, no wonder the disease is becoming rampant."

"Yes, well, very sorry I am for them. But God forbid we get the cholera from them." Edward sounded fearful. "Anyway, Weavers Flour Mill Warehouse on the next dock are taking on strong workers. The pay and conditions, are much better than we are getting now. So, come with me tonight James, to the Farmers Arms, in Frog Street. George Davies and some of the boys from Weavers, meet there for a drink every Friday," Edward said excitedly. "We are to meet Mr Dewy Lloyd, the brother-in-law of Mr Harold Morris. Mr. Morris has kindly recommended me and you for jobs, to Mr Lloyd, who is some sort of high up in Weavers." James agreed and without hesitation.

That evening the cousins were approaching the Farmers Arms and just about to pass the infirmary, when James stopped suddenly. Coming out of the infirmary was the woman he could never forget.

"Hello, Emma," he blurted out. "Oh, I mean Mrs MacIndow."

"Do I know you, sir?" she asked. "Your face is familiar, but I am sorry, I cannot recollect."

"James Owen, my family and I stayed at your house for the Eisteddfod," he said speaking with perfect English, which the Reverend Thomas

Richards would approve of. "I hope you are well ma'am."

"Yes of course, now I remember, but you were just a young boy. I can hardly recognise you," she replied. "As for me, I am well thank you. I have just been visiting a friend who is ill. How are your family, all well I hope?"

At this point Edward saw George Davies, coming towards them, so Edward tapped James, on the shoulder. "Yes, yes thank you for asking. This is my cousin, Edward, and we are on our way to meet someone important at the Farmers Arms, concerning employment," said James hurriedly.

"Well I will say goodbye, and delay you no more," she replied. "It was very nice to meet you again."

James, with a heavy heart, said goodbye and watched her walk away. "How come you know the lovely widow then, James?" asked George as they walked towards the Inn.

"Widow?" asked James in shock. "I didn't know she was a widow."

"Well yes," replied George. "Her husband, David MacIndow, died at sea two years ago. We'd better make a move on now James. We don't want to be late."

The Farmers Arms, being a popular venue for the working men of Swansea, was very crowded when the young men arrived. The air was thick with tobacco smoke and smelled of beer and body odour. Sawdust was scattered over the floor and the walls were damp with condensation. Nevertheless, the cheerful atmosphere created by contented men, obliterated their surroundings.

A voice calling Edward led the cousins to a table near the window where a group of men sat. George Davies introduced James and Edward, and offered the cousins the two chairs which he had kept empty for them. "Will you have something to drink boys? Before I take you in to the private room to meet Mr. Lloyd?" asked George.

"No thanks, George," replied Edward. "I think we had better stay sober until after we've seen the boss."

"Good thinking, Edward," said George. "Come on then, I'll take you straight in."

The private room was a vast improvement with regard to cleanliness, and though the air was thick with tobacco smoke, it came from the pleasing fragrance of expensive cigars. "Mr. Lloyd," George addressed a very smartly dressed gentleman who sat with several important looking men, in the centre of the room. "I have brought Edward and James, who have an appointment to meet you."

"Thank you, George," replied Mr Lloyd. "Come on over to the small table by the window boys, so we can have a talk." He spoke with a common accent, which surprised James.

'*He's not one of your cultured Swansea Jacks, for all his posh clothes,*' thought James, as they followed Mr Lloyd to the chosen table.

"Right then, boys," said Mr Lloyd. "I think I've heard enough about you two from my good friend and brother-in-law. So, I'll tell you a bit about me and the work. I have grafted boy and man, all my life to get where I am today. So, that's what I want to see from my workers. Work hard, keep your noses clean, and you will do all right. Start shirking off and you'll be out faster than a bat out of hell." He smiled but, gave each boy a searching glance before he continued with, "You both look strong enough to hump and stack the flour bales, which is where you'll start, next week. 'Cos I will be away on Monday, you will go to my man in charge, Tommy Davies. Come to think of it, you might well find him in the outside room, having a drink with the lads." He ended with a dismissive wave towards the door.

Returning to the public room, Edward led James to the table where George and his mates were sitting. "Everything all right then, boys?" asked George.

"Oh yes," replied Edward with a grin. "We are to start on Monday."

"That's grand then," said George. "Come and sit down while I tell you who's who by here. Introducing his companions George began with Big Dai and Little Dai who were seated either side of him. Both men were of slim build, however, one was taller by almost a foot. Sitting next to little Dai was Young Henry, a jolly looking lad, who seemed to be wearing a permanent grin beneath laughing blue eyes. "Henry is the warehouse joker," said George. "He never stops telling us what his mammy says, *'If someone hasn't got a smile give them one of yours.'*" This was followed by a chorus of laughter from the table, which made young Henry blush and stutter "Oh shut up you lot."

"Nothing wrong with listening to your mammy, boy." said the tough looking man sitting next to him, who was introduced as Bryan Rees. Bryan's gentle speech contrasted with his appearance, which was that of a burly lout.

"Bryan is the Warehouse hard man, boys, nobody messes with Bryan. But, he's the best man to have in your corner when trouble starts," said George. "He soon stopped the lads calling young Henry, a mammy's boy, and he's settled loads of other scores too."

"Give your mouth a rest now, George," said the last man at the table. He looked to be several years older than the others, and sounded more mature.

"As you might have noticed, George is the works' jabber mouth. Whatever you want to know ask George. I'm Ben Jenkins, and before he has a go at me, there's nothing more to say. So, make a start on the ale we got in for you and we'll all have a good night."

Edward sat and took up his pint of ale. James also sat down but, before beginning his drink he turned to the boys, saying, "Mr Lloyd told us to see the chargehand, Tommy Davies, because he won't be there on Monday. If he's in here will you point him out to us?"

"Oh Tommy, yes he's over by there with that crowd near the door. He's the sour looking one with the bald head," said Henry. "Don't tell him I said that mind, because he's more than a bit touchy about his head, and nobody wants to be on the wrong side of that loony." Looking up James met the eyes of the man described by Henry. '*He's been told about us,*' thought James, '*and while I'm looking him over he's doing the same to us.*' James nodded in acknowledgement, hoping the gesture would provide a positive reaction from Tommy. On the contrary, ignoring James' action, Tommy, with a stony look, turned back to his companions. James had no alternative but to return his attention to the men at his table.

Monday morning when the cousins met Tommy Davies, his blunt features showed no change. Edward introduced them both and was given the abrupt reply, "Come on then, I'll show you around and tell you what's what, then you just get on with it." During the day the cousins had little time for talk with George and the others. They both coped with the hard work, though they later described it as 'back breaking'. But, by the end of the first week they had become accustomed to the routine. And, although they felt exhausted, their wage packets proved to be adequate compensation.

James formed a habit of joining his workmates on a Friday evening at the Farmers Arms. Each time he passed the infirmary he thought of Emma, hoping to see her again.

Three weeks passed before his persistence was rewarded. She was walking down the steps outside the infirmary, but, her beautiful face looked drawn and tear-stained. She looked up and saw James. Making an obvious effort to compose herself she said, "Oh, James, it's you, I'm sorry, I can't talk right now."

"Let me help you?" James blurted out. "I can't leave you like this."

"No, no, thank you," she replied. "I have just left the bedside of a very dear friend who passed away just minutes ago."

"That is very sad, and awful for you." Concern for her echoed in his voice. "Would you let me to take you up to the Mackworth Hotel, where we could have some tea? Perhaps you should not be alone for a while."

"Why, how kind you are!" she said, surprised that this young man should care about her. "But I can't burden you with a weak tearful woman."

"Say no more," he replied. "I remember how you looked after me when I was a boy." He paused. "And my family too," he added in haste.

"Well now, there is nothing more I can do here." she was feeling a little calmer as she continued thoughtfully "My Aunt Alice is looking after my children, and I don't feel like delivering the bad news just yet. So I think I will accept your kind offer."

"Good for you," said a delighted James, trying his best to sound solicitous. "It's just a short walk. Please take my arm." The Mackworth Hotel, a venue favoured by the genteel families of the locality, was situated in a prime position on Swansea High Street. They arrived at the tea rooms, which were annexed at the side of the hotel lobby, and found an empty table. James ordered a pot of tea for two, which was promptly brought to their table by a very pleasant serving girl. Emma, having refused the offer of cake, did manage to nibble on one of the dainty biscuits from her saucer.

At first they talked as polite strangers but both gradually relaxed and began to exchange confidences about their lives. When James related comical events about his youngest sisters, Emma was impressed by the affection in his voice. "Children can be such a joy, I know my two can make me laugh one minute and drive me to distraction the next," she said with a smile. As time went on Emma became more aware that this man was dangerously attractive! She felt herself blushing at the thought. James, sensing good vibes coming from her, decided to take advantage of the moment.

"There's is to be a seaside outing in two weeks-time, when the men and women from Weavers are invited to take their families. As I don't have family in Swansea would you like to come, as my guest, and bring your children?" James asked, tongue in cheek, "I'm told these trips are a real fun day out," he added hastily.

She was silent for a few minutes, deep in thought. "I don't know if that would be wise, James. Me being a widow and you a single man, though I know my children would be over the moon." She paused again before adding, "Let me think about this and maybe I will see what my mother and father think. That might sound a bit unusual coming from a woman of my age. Because people will gossip and I would hate to upset them, they are so good to me. In fact, I don't know what I would have done without them since I lost my husband."

James thought for just a minute. "Oh yes I hadn't thought like that, maybe your aunt, the one who baby sits, could come with us, what do you think of that?" James suggested.

"As a sort of chaperone you mean?" Emma couldn't help smiling as she answered. "Well my aunt Alice is the youngest of my father's family — in fact she is only ten years older than me — and she is very young at heart. Let me think about this James, give me a week, maybe you could call next Saturday afternoon, and I will let you know." Over an hour had gone by, and Emma suddenly realised, by the way he looked at her, that there was more than kindness in his gaze. She felt warmness in her heart, that she had thought gone when her husband David died. *'What is the matter with me?'* she thought. *'I hardly know this man. Because he is tall, muscular and handsome, any woman would find him attractive. His deep grey eyes are fascinating. But I need to put these thoughts away, I am a vulnerable widow with two children, and he is too young for me anyway.'*

Meanwhile, James was content. He was sitting next to his boyhood dream. Gazing at her beautiful face, he began to fantasise, longing to take her in his arms, and make love to her.

Accepting the position she was in, Emma decided that she must be the one to show common sense. She slowly stood saying, "Thank you so much for this evening, James, I am more than ready now to face my aunt's questions."

James awoke abruptly from his reverie and stood with her. "Oh, don't mention it. I will see you safely home before we say good night."

Not knowing how to refuse his offer without giving offence, Emma accepted his arm as they walked from the tea rooms. They were both silent and lost in thought until they arrived at her house. She thanked him again before shaking his hand, saying goodnight and closing her door. James walked back to his lodgings in a daze, he knew he was in love with this woman of his dreams.

Meantime Emma arrived home to find her aunt waiting anxiously. "Sorry I've been so long, Alice," Emma said sorrowfully. "Jane died today, I know it was expected, but I was still upset. When I was coming from the infirmary, I bumped into an old friend and he very kindly took me tea."

"He?" exclaimed Alice with a questioning tone. Emma blushed and felt uncomfortable as she explained who James was. "Right then, there's more to this than meets the eye," said Alice insightfully. "We have always been more like sisters than aunt and niece, so you should be able to talk freely with me, my lovely."

Emma thought for a moment, after having spent a day of suppressed emotions, she could no longer contain herself. So, she decided to confide in Alice. Beginning with the sad loss of her friend, she went on to describe her meeting with James. How kind he was when she was so upset. Finally she came to his invitation for her and the children to his works day out. "What you think Alice, because I feel might have given rise to gossip already. Having tea with a man on my own, and our family set such store by respectability. Also, I rely on my mother and father — you know how generous Dad is to me," said Emma, emphasising the word respectability, then she paused, blushing again as she continued, " And the thing is, to be honest with you, certain feelings are there, you know, attractions between us. He did suggest that you might come with us as a sort of chaperone, but well, I don't know what to do."

"Emma, you're babbling, just stop for a minute and think. You're still a very lovely young woman, and there's not that much of an age difference. I'm sure your mother and father would think like me

119

and be glad for you to have some pleasure. And as for the money, well, your father is hardly short of a bob or two, we both know he has plenty," Alice said firmly. "Also what life have you seen? Married at sixteen, two children before you were twenty, and your husband away at sea most of the time. Then being widowed at such an early age, you deserve a bit of life, my dear. Besides, I know it's early days, but if a relationship did blossom, well there's nothing wrong with that. You've been a widow long enough to have earned everyone's respect, and your children could do with a man around." She stopped for a moment and grinned, "What's more, I'm sure we'd all enjoy the day out. I know I would."

"You make it all sound all right, Alice, and I suppose if you do come as well there could be no objections. I mean to say, it's just a day out after all," said Emma, breathing a sigh of relief. Although she was not totally convinced she was doing the right thing, she desperately wanted to see James again.

"That sounds good to me," said Alice. "If you like I will come down next Saturday and be here when he arrives. With me here you can call him in for a cup of tea with clear conscience. To tell you the truth I am dying to meet him. But I won't be a kill joy mind you, I can spend a little time in the kitchen making the tea. Then if you like, I will take young Violet out the garden for a bit of tidying up. Tom, I know, will be at cricket." When Emma gave her a hesitant nod of approval, Alice was content with what she felt was a sensible conclusion. "Right then, I must be off now, I will see you tomorrow my dear." That night Emma tossed and turned in her bed. Trying as hard as she could, she found it impossible to banish thoughts of James and the feelings he had aroused in her heart.

The following week passed agonisingly slowly for James. The men talked of the coming outing, but James remained silent on the subject. He was not prepared to confide in anyone until he had an answer from Emma. However, Friday evening, Edward was ready to go to the Farmers Arms when James decided it was necessary to confide in his cousin, the main reason being that James did not intend to join the men that night, because he wanted to bathe and get himself ready for the morrow. On hearing James' plans Edward was for a while nonplussed. "Well you've kept me in the dark cousin. I thought you had a bit of a glint in your eye the night we met her in town, but I made no more of it." He became serious before he continued with, "I hope you know what you're doing James. She's not a young girl to be toyed with, and her father is a prominent man. Besides she's years older than you with two kids already."

"I know all that Edward, but I also know how I feel about her, and I just can't help myself," James answered impatiently. "This is not a passing fancy, this is the woman I want to be with for the rest of my life."

"Right then, if you're that sure, you'd better prepare yourself for the bit of stick that is bound to come," said Edward. "For a start, if she says yes to the outing, you're going to have to tell Tommy Davies who you want to bring. And that nasty bugger is going to have something not so clever to say. He's been asking for a good hiding from more than one person that I can think of. Be ready for it from him and maybe from others. You're going to need a plenty of control over your temper, or you'll put the tin hat on everything. Don't forget that Tommy can get you the sack and then where will you be?"

"Yes, I guess you're right." James thought for a few seconds before saying, "But they, Tommy or whoever they are, can say what they like about me, but they'd better not put her down, that's all I have to say. Now off you go and enjoy yourself and leave me to my supper. And then I am going to take a bath and get rid of this beard growth," he added rubbing his rough chin.

James rose early on Saturday morning, unable to enjoy his weekly 'lie in'. He decided to go for a swim in the sea. A strong swimmer, James often enjoyed 'a dip' in Swansea bay. He thought this was a good way to pass the time before he got ready to visit Emma.

He arrived at Emma's house to find she had company. The person with her was expensively dressed and looked every inch a lady. Even though she was taller than Emma, James stood over her. "James I would like you to meet my Aunt Alice. Alice, this is James Owen, the man I told you who was so kind to me," she said and smiled at James who looked a little uncomfortable. However, he shook Alice by the hand and told her how pleased he was to meet her. He felt much easier when Alice smiled warmly at him, saying that she also was very pleased to meet the man who had shown her niece such kindness.

"Shall I go and make a cup of tea then, Emma, while you talk to James?" said Alice, not waiting for an answer as she made her way to the kitchen.

"Sit yourself down on the big armchair, James and we can talk," said Emma trying desperately to slow down her beating heart. The feelings he invoked in her was making this very difficult.

"Thank you, Emma," James replied as he took the proffered seat. "I hope you have been well since our last meeting." He was reluctant to broach the subject he had come to discuss, in case she was to turn him down. And he wanted to spend as much time as possible with her.

"Yes, I have thank you, very well." She paused, collecting her thoughts, during which there was an awkward silence. James sat on the edge of his chair, waiting for what he thought was going to be rejection.

The silence was broken by the simultaneous entrance of Emma's daughter Violet, and Alice with a tray of tea and Welsh cakes. Emma thanked Alice for the tea and introduced Violet to James and vice versa. "I brought you and your mother a few plants," said Alice turning to Violet. "But the garden will need a bit of tidying up first. Will you come out and give me a hand?"

Left alone James and Emma were silent, while Emma poured the teas from a china teapot. "I think I remember rightly James, that you take milk but no sugar," said Emma shyly, taking note that Alice had used her best china teapot, cups and saucers.

"Yes, thank you," replied James, so pleased that she remembered this small detail from their last meeting.

"I've thought long and hard about the forthcoming outing, James, and I've had a talk with Alice," said Emma, causing James to sit further forward and put his tea down on the small table in front of him.

"The children, Alice and I will be happy to join you if you are still of a mind to invite us."

James couldn't refrain from grinning widely as he told her how delighted he was at her decision.

"I do know Bethan, Edward's girlfriend and some of the wives who are going. In fact, one is the mother of my Thomas' good friend," said Emma. "She told me that the women take picnics, and I will be pleased to do this for us." Gradually losing her shyness, Emma continued with, "I don't know anything about your tastes, James. What would you like me to bring?"

'Who cares about food,' thought James. *'I just want you there,'* but he said, "Don't worry about me Emma, I'm not a fussy eater — anything you choose will be fine by me."

Emma had now relaxed and she began a general conversation by asking James about his work colleagues who would be going on the outing. James complied, grateful that most of the men going with them were of good repute, unlike some he worked with. He in turn asked her about her family and friends. Alice and Violet returned to find them conversing amiably.

James rose about to take his leave when Alice said, "Don't let us disturb you. Violet and I have to go and wash our dirty hands."

"Well I was just about to go anyway," said James, reluctantly rising.

Emma rose to see him out saying, "Alice, the children and I will look forward to seeing you again for the outing, James."

While walking towards his lodgings James was deep in thought. He needed to think of a way to tell Tommy Davies without prompting an unacceptable remark.

By Monday morning he had decided on a slightly devious approach. Tommy was coming out of the boss's office when James arrived. "I need the rest of the names of everybody who is going on the outing," he said loudly to the men in the room. "Right now, or you can all forget it." He was holding a list in his hand when he continued, "Howells, the two Joneses and the Owens. Come on then, I haven't got all day."

James waited until the others had finished before he approached Tommy. "I've got a few names to put down," said James. "As I've got nobody in Swansea, I am taking friends of my family — Miss Alice Davies, her niece Mrs Emma MacIndow and her two children." As James had hoped there was no cutting remark Tommy, who simply wrote down the names James had given him.

"That was clever, the way you put Alice first, James boy," Edward remarked later. "But you are still going to face the music. That is, unless you can hide that daft, lovesick look, in front of the boys."

"Yea, right," said James seriously. "I can take our mates ribbing, I just hope that bloody Tommy keeps his mouth shut. And that nothing is said in front of her and her kids."

"You needn't worry about anybody, even Tommy, being stupid enough to say anything out of the way in front of your Emma." said Edward. "Our boys wouldn't anyway, and Tommy would be too scared to cause aggro' in front of the boss. You know how butter wouldn't melt in his mouth when Mr Lloyd is around, and Mrs Lloyd will be there too."

Edwards's words turned out to be true. The day of the outing was a great success for James and his party. Swansea bay was at its best, the sun shone on the golden sands, and the surf rose and fell smoothly. There was a chill in the air, which made the ladies forbid the small children to venture into the sea.

James with some of the men organized games for the children. Emma's son Thomas was impressed with James, who played cricket with the boys, while Violet and a few of the older girls made sandcastles with little ones.

Later the boss handed round a bottle of beer each to the men, and they sat on the sand enjoying a drink, whilst the women chatted amiably as they prepared the picnics. They divided into groups to eat their food. Edward, and his girlfriend Beth, joined James' group. Beth, being a good friend of Emma's niece, was well known to her and to Alice, and they both liked the young couple. James was very careful to avoid paying too much attention to Emma. Fortunately he found Alice easy to talk to, and young Thomas demanded much of his attention. Even though he had no chance to talk to Emma alone, the occasional glance, and returning smile was enough to tell him that she was enjoying herself. They were eating their food when a cry went out. "Help, help us, somebody help!"

James and Edward both rose swiftly when they saw two of the older boys, floundering in the sea. One of the boys was going under, and the other, who was shouting for help, was trying to save his friend.

James threw off his shirt as he ran, with Edward following closely. The boys were out of their depth, but within one hundred yards of the shore. Swimming with strong fast strokes James soon reached the boys. However, the weaker boy had gone under the water, and was by then out of sight. The other boy seemed exhausted, but was sensibly lying on his back, floating. James took a deep breath and dived under. He reached the drowning boy, and brought him to the surface. Taking a strong grip he turned the prone lad onto his back. He swam, using one arm, dragging the boy with the other hand gripping the boy's chin.

The boys' fathers and several other men were in the water heading towards them. Edward had seen the first boy safely to his parents, before he also turned to help James, who actually would have been better off without interference.

When he came to within his depth James stood and carried the boy to big Dai, the boy's father. They walked to the beach and sat the boy on the sand. He was spluttering and coughing up sea water, but thanks to James' quick actions he had survived. Crowds had gathered on the shore and Mr Dewy Lloyd, who had also run into the water to help, took charge. "Everybody back off now, give them some breathing space," he shouted. "The boys are all right, so we can all go back and enjoy ourselves."

Meantime James had flopped onto the sand next to big Dai and his boy, and the boy's mother, Elsie, who had joined them. "What the hell were you thinking of Bobby?" big Dai said to his son, while tapping the boy's back. "Bloody young fool, showing off, nearly got you drowned. Besides worrying your poor mother to a nervous breakdown, and her supposed to be having a nice day out."

"Take it easy Dai, the boy has already learnt a hard lesson," said James to his friend. "I think he's coughed up all the bad stuff now. So why don't you take him, and your poor upset wife, up the sands to have a drink of good water."

"Jesus, James, I don't know what to say to you, and you just saved the life of my boy." Big Dai offered James his hand. "Me and mine will always be in your debt my friend."

"Go on with you, Dai," James responded with a firm handshake. "I just happened to get to him first, you and the others were right behind me." He had hardly finished speaking, when big Dai's wife caught him in a bear hug. "Thank you, from a grateful mother," said the tearful woman. She laid a smacking kiss on James' cheek before turning back to her son.

Then a gorgeous young woman put her arms around James, saying. "Thanks from me too, for saving my little brother."

Emma, who had been standing nearby, watched with sinking heart, as this lovely girl embraced a half-naked James.

Mr Dewy Lloyd was next to approach James. "That was a damn good thing you did boy. Brave as well 'cos a drowning man could take you down with him."

"Not me sir, I've been swimming since I was a young lad, the water holds no fear for me," James replied. "I once saw a father rescue his son like that, and he showed me and the other boys with me, what to do. After that we used to make a game of rescuing each other. But, I must be honest, I never thought I would have to do it for real, "Mr Lloyd smiled and nodded, and tapping James' shoulder he caught sight of Emma, and Alice. "Good day to you ladies," he said. "How nice to see you both at our little outing. Please to give my respects to your good brother, Miss Davies," he said to Alice, and off he went to join his own group. Alice passed James a towel saying, "You'd best dry yourself off a bit James."

James thanked her, and then looked around to find Edward, who was enjoying the praise of his lovely girlfriend Beth. Workmates were patting Edward on the back and grinning with one exception. Tommy Davies had stood back scowling. *'There's going to be a reckoning between me and him one of these days,'* thought James.

Catching James' eye Edward waved and taking Beth by the hand he walked to his cousin calling, "We'd better go and get out of these wet clothes now, James."

"Right you are," James replied. "At least we had our shirts off so they are dry."

Looking around at Emma, James suddenly felt uneasy, she had not said one word to him, and she was avoiding eye contact with him.

"Will you forgive us, Emma, if Edward and I go off and get dry clothes?" James enquired, giving Emma a searching look.

"Yes, of course." She was horrified with herself, but unable to stop blushing as she spoke.

"Come on then, James," said Edward. "We will not be long girls."

The cousins hurried back to their lodgings, and changed into dry clothes. But by the time they returned to the beach, they found that everyone was packing up to leave.

James immediately joined Emma. "Let me help you with that basket, Emma." he said stooping to take hold of the basket. Emma was also doing so, when their hands touched, and their eyes met! Emma withdrew her hand and looked away quickly, but not before they each felt electricity flow on the contact of hands.

James was confused by Emma's reaction. *'Did she find my touch repulsive, or did she feel pleasure like me?'* he thought. Further contemplation was impossible because Alice was saying, "If we're already now, I for one am ready to get back for a nice hot cup of tea. What about you, James? I hope you will join us."

"Thank you, Alice. That would be very nice," James responded. "As long as it, all right with you, Emma." he added, looking at Emma for approval.

"Yes, of course, you are welcome," said Emma. Again avoiding eye contact with James, she looked over his shoulder and said to Beth, "You and Edward must come as well, dear. Now, Thomas, you can go and call Violet. She is still sitting on that sand dune with her friends."

"Wait for me then, James," said Thomas. "I will carry one side of the basket with you."

"Right, Thomas," James replied, replied smiling. "So, hurry up then." When Thomas and Violet returned the whole group made their way to Emma's house. They drank tea and finished the contents of the picnic basket. After which Beth pointed out that it was getting late so, they should be making their way home. James felt as if he too would be expected to leave, then he had an idea. "Yes, you're right, but before I go..." He paused looking at Thomas. "What about you and me Thomas, clear up for the ladies."

Alice stepped in quickly before Emma could object. "Well that's an offer not to be refused," she said. "Violet, would you walk with Beth and Edward as far as Granny's house, and tell her about today."

When James and Thomas were in the kitchen, Alice, sitting next to Emma asked, "Right, what's going on now? I know there's something wrong."

"Alice," Emma replied. "It's no good. I saw that lovely young girl with James, today and I knew then, I just have to forget him."

"Is that all?" said Alice. "You were jealous. Perfectly natural, when a pretty girl, makes up to the man you're falling in love with. But think again, please, Emma, he is obviously crazy about *you*."

Emma had no time to reply because Thomas called from the kitchen, "Mama, where is a towel to wipe the dishes?"

"Right I'm coming," she replied. She rose when Alice caught her arm saying, "Try being nice my dear,"

Emma just nodded in agreement, and smiled, as she walked to the kitchen," I will help James with clearing up, Thomas," said Emma to her son. "Because you will need to get your things ready for your Sunday school. Then it will be time for bed."

Left alone, Emma handed James a tea towel saying, "I haven't had chance, before this, to say thank you for today James."

Deciding it was time to speak his piece, James said "I thought at one time you were upset about something, Emma. I hope it was nothing I said, or did?"

"Oh no, James," she said, and looking into his anxious grey eyes, she had to fight back the tears which were threatening. "It was nothing. Please just forget it."

"Now I can see your upset," said James. Putting his hands on her shoulders, he gently drew her into his arms. "My dear Emma, can't you tell me what is wrong? You must know by now how I feel about you, I would die rather than hurt you."

Emma laid her head against his chest, and she could feel his rapidly beating heart. She raised her face, offering her lips invitingly.

James bent his head and kissed her, tenderly at first. When he felt her responding, his kisses became more passionate.

Emma drew back, she could feel he was aroused, and a voice in her head was saying. *'Thomas and Alice are in the next room, you must put a stop to this right now!'* "James," Emma whispered in his ear. "We must remember that we are not alone. Come with me back into the sitting room, before Thomas comes to say goodnight."

When they walked in Alice looked up from the book she had started to read. Smiling at them both she said, "I am for the off now Emma. Thomas has said goodnight to me, and he will want to say goodnight to James. So, I'll just thank you again for today James, and goodnight to you both."

Alice was about to leave when Violet came rushing in. "Gran sent me down to say can I stay the night. Grandpa is still out, and I can keep her company?"

Without waiting for an answer, she kissed her mother on the cheek and said, "Goodnight then, goodnight James, goodnight Alice."

"Wait for me," Alice said to the girl. "I'll walk with you, James is waiting to say goodnight to Thomas." Emma, while walking Alice and Violet to the door, whispered in her aunt's ear, "I know what you're up to you devil."

"Good night, James, good night, Emma." Alice called smiling.

Returning to her sitting room, Emma had mixed feelings. Was she cross or pleased with Alice? She sat next to James in silence. "I need to speak to you now, Emma, before Thomas joins us."

James, taking her hand spoke softly. "I love you and I know you are the only woman for me.

Please tell me how you feel towards me. If you cannot return my feelings, tell me now, and I will not bother you again."

"But James, you hardly know me, we hardly know each other," was her response.

"I know how I feel, my love." he said softly. "Just tell me, just put me out of my misery. Do I go now and leave you alone, or is there a chance for us?"

Emma looked into his deep grey eyes and she was defeated. "Oh yes, James, I have strong feelings for you. But, there is the age difference and the fact that I have two children. And James, after what you did today, you will have all the girls chasing you."

"The age difference is nothing to me," he said. "And your children are part of you so I will love them too. I want no other woman but you, my love, but I don't want to rush you into anything." He paused, then seeing her smile he grinned and added, " Just say you'll marry me tomorrow."

They were wrapped in each other's arms when Thomas came into the room. "Mammy!" Thomas exclaimed. "Are you two getting married?"

"Thomas! Will you please calm down," said his mother as she and James hastily drew apart. "As for me and James, well now there's a lot for me to think about, before I answer your question. I will need to talk to Violet, and you, son. Also, I must speak to your Grandmother and Grandfather."

"Would you mind Thomas, if your mother was to marry me?" James asked the boy.

"Oh no, James, I think that would be good," Thomas replied. "You can be my new father then, can't you?"

"Wait just a minute you two, everything is moving too fast," said Emma sternly. "I promise you both, I will think hard. So, for now that will have to do. Not another word to anyone, Thomas, not to anyone, understand?"

"Yes, Mama all right then," her son replied.

James and I need to talk, so we can all have cocoa and then you must go to bed," she said to Thomas seriously. "You've had enough excitement for one day, and you have to get up for chapel in the morning."

Emma made the hot cocoa in record time, and James talked about cricket to Thomas who then went off to bed without complaint. *'Alone at last,'* thought James. He took Emma's hand saying, "Emma, I must know, how do you feel about me?"

"Oh James, wise or foolish I don't know, but I do love you," she responded. "She loves me!"

He exclaimed, lifting her up with his hands around her tiny waist, and twirling her around. Then loosening his hold she slithered down his body to the ground. Their bodies were as one, when he looked into her eyes saying, "Emma, my love, will you marry me?"

"Yes, James, I will marry you," she said, adding with a smile. "But maybe tomorrow will be a bit too soon, don't you think?" They laughed together, kissed and exchanged words of love. This time, when she knew that he was aroused, she didn't stop him, she felt almost wanton, in her desire for him.

They made love, taking delight in each other's bodies, and eventually falling asleep in each other's arms.

James was the first to stir, when the sun came up, shining through the window. He woke her with a kiss. "I really have to go my dear, and get changed for work."

"James? Oh, James!" she said, waking with a start. "Last night…"

"Stop there my love," he said cutting her short. "I'm not one for fancy speeches, but I know that last night was between two people who love each other. And we will be married as soon as you say the word. For now though, I have to drag myself away and go to work. I will be back tonight, when we can make plans for our future together." James kissed and hugged her before forcing himself to leave her. Emma hurriedly rose and got dressed.

Making a determined effort to put the ecstatic experiences of last night out of mind, she concentrated on tidying the room.

Later that day Emma confided in Alice. Without revealing all, she told her aunt that James had proposed and that she had accepted. Alice was surprised that the relationship had progressed so rapidly, nevertheless she was delighted to see her niece so happy. Alice persuaded her, even though she was no longer in need of their permission, she should speak to her parents soon and of course her children. Knowing that Alice's advice was sound Emma resolved to speak to James about a visit to her mother and father as soon as possible. When James arrived that evening, Violet and Thomas were both at home with Emma.

"Hello. Have you said anything to the children, Emma?" was James' opening question.

"I had to, James. Thomas made it impossible for me to delay any longer. He has more or less decided our fate for us." Emma replied "This means we must see my parents without delay, James. Will you come with me tomorrow?"

"Of course I will, dear, and so for now, please stop worrying."

As arranged James called for Emma the following evening. However, he was feeling nervous about confronting her parents with their plans. He was sure they would try to talk her out of marrying him.

On hearing their daughter's news, both Lewis and Edith reacted as Alice had done. "Surely you haven't known each other long enough to warrant such a big step. Only a matter of a month or two isn't it?" Lewis said. "I would advise you to hold your horses, maybe until this time next year."

"We have both made the big decision after careful thought Lewis," James replied. "The obvious objections, such as my age and the fact that Emma has two children by a previous marriage, can be forgotten. Neither matters to me. I love her and her children, Lewis. I promise you I will always care for them as best I can."

"As for me, Dad," Emma added, "I know I can trust this man with my happiness, and that of my children. Why, Thomas worships him already, and Violet likes him very much. A whole year is I feel too long for us to wait , maybe six months. And then we could plan for a spring wedding."

CHAPTER 6
1875 - 1876

James and Emma were married on the twelfth of March 1875. Eight months later, their first child was born, in November 1875. A sweet little girl they named **Amy**. Amy was just over two months old when Emma discovered she was pregnant again. James and Emma, who both loved children were delighted. James was earning a decent wage, which enabled them to live comfortably. When he married Emma, James had insisted on taking full financial, and physical responsibility, for Emma, Violet and Thomas. Lewis Davies, Emma's father, had, prior to their marriage, supported Emma and her children.

The second of November 1876 was to prove a date, which James would never forget. Emma gave birth to their second child, in the early hours of that momentous Monday — a fine healthy boy, who they named David Lewis, David after James' father and Lewis after Emma's father

James was a proud and happy man when he arrived at work that day. He was telling his mates the good news and received slaps on his back, congratulations and best wishes, when along came Tommy Davies. "What the bloody hell is going on here?" said Tommy fiercely. "No bloody work. That, I can see."

"We were just taking a minute to congratulate James on the birth of his son," Bryan Rees replied quickly, but with ominous calm. "Now we'll get to work, right boys?" The rest of the men had remained silent, all waiting to see if Tommy was willing to stand up to Bryan. However, after a nod from the hard man, they got back to their work.

Tommy, knowing he had been ousted, was furious. "So it's another brat for your old woman is it then, Owen?" he said to James, sneering and emphasising the word old.

James 'saw red' and lashed out, delivering a brutal right hook to Tommy's chin. Landing on his back, almost a yard away, Tommy was lying still. "Jesus, he's out cold," said little Dai, who stood over the prone Tommy.

Meantime Bryan, sensing James' anger, had tried, but was too late to hold his friend back. "Oh my God, James boy, you have done it now," he said. "He asked for it," James replied, still angry. "In fact he's been asking for it for years."

Then Ben Jenkins took charge saying, "Henry run and get some water, the rest of you get back to work as if you saw nothing." Henry was returning with a cup of water when he almost bumped into the boss.

"What's going on here, young Henry?" asked Mr Lloyd. "Somebody need water then?"

"Ur um yes, sir," replied Henry stuttering. "It it's for Mr Davies, sir."

"Tommy?" asked Mr Lloyd sounding surprised. When Henry simply nodded, he said, "Well come on then let's go, I'll come too."

Tommy opened his eyes to see Mr Lloyd, Ben and young Henry standing over him. "Drink a drop of water, Tommy." said Ben. "It will make you feel better."

Tommy took the water and after drinking his fill he turned to his boss. "Mr Lloyd, this is all Owen's doing, the man's lost the plot," said Tommy, after some quick thinking. "He came at me for no reason, going berserk."

"James Owen," called out Mr Lloyd. "My office, now, and you had better come too Tommy. The rest of you get on with your work."

"Right then," said Mr Lloyd as he sat behind his big desk "Let's hear what you have to say. You first, James, as it's you who has been accused of going mad."

"The man insulted me and my wife, sir, and I could not let that go." James replied.

"Rubbish," Tommy interrupted. "I did nothing of the sort."

"Hold your horses now, Tommy," said Mr Lloyd. "I was not asking you to speak yet. What exactly was said, James?"

"Well, sir," replied James thoughtfully. "The boys were congratulating me on the birth of my son this morning. When Tommy interrupted saying, I'd given another brat to an old woman."

"I see.," said the boss frowning. "So, what do you say to that Tommy?"

"Well now, I did say the old woman, meaning the wife. I have often heard the men call their wives the old woman," said the crafty chargehand.

"Right then," said Mr Lloyd. "I want you both to go back to work while I give this matter some thought."

"It was almost the end of their working day, when Mr Lloyd approached James. "I'll see you now, James," he said, before turning to his chargehand. "Wait behind after work Tommy, I will want a word with you before you go."

When they were alone in his office Mr Lloyd said to James, "You two have put me in hell of a position. Especially as I know your wife to be a real lady, who should receive respect. But I can't close my eyes to an attack on my chargehand. Nobody knows better than me, that Tommy Davies can be a right bastard. He is about to get hell of a bollocking from me, but, he keeps the men working. So, sorry as I am to do this, it's you I'm going to have to let you go, James. I've made your wages up to the end of the week, and I've put in an extra weeks pay. But, I think it's best if you finish now." James was lost for words, everything had happened too quickly. He left the boss' office in a daze.

Edward and some of his workmates were waiting outside for James. "How did it go with the boss then, James?" Edward asked.

"I've been given the push, just like that, out on my ear," James answered dully.

"Oh, bloody hell," Bryan exclaimed. "Sorry, we are James, come and have a drink with us boys then, before you go home."

"Just a minute, Bryan," said the ever sensible Ben. "He has bad news to take home. I don't think it would be a good idea for him to deliver it smelling of booze."

"No, no, your quite right, Ben," James answered. "But thank you for the thought, boys."

Big Dai laid his hand on James' shoulder saying, "Come on, James boy, let's go."

James and big Dai, being neighbours, habitually walked home together. "If there's anything me and the boys can do, James," said Edward.

"I know cousin, and thanks," James replied nodding, as he and big Dai left. As they walked big Dai spoke to James in a voice full of hate. "That bastard, Tommy, has not got away with this, he'll regret this day."

James looked surprised at the tone used by this gentle giant. He shook his head not knowing how to reply this outburst by his friend. Still feeling somewhat stunned he remained silent.

James arrived home to find Alice making dinner, and his mother-in-law nursing his son. Both ladies said their hellos, beaming at James. "Come and say hello to your son, James," his mother-in-law said, holding up the baby. "Emma has just fed him and I took over for her to have a rest."

James looked down at his son, all the pride and happiness he had felt that morning was gone. He could feel nothing but regret for his impulsive reaction to Tommy's taunts. *'If only I could turn the clock back,'* he thought. "Are you all right, James?" said Alice coming out of the kitchen.

"Yes, I'm all right, Alice," answered James. "But, I'd better go and get cleaned up before I hold him, Edith," he said sadly, to his mother-in-law.

James was making his way out of the room when he stopped. "The thing is, you should hear it from me, before the gossips start," James said suddenly. "I lost my job today. Now, I will go and clean up and then I'll go up to Emma."

The awkward silence was broken by Alice. "I'm so sorry you lost your job, James. But do you think you could wait a while before you tell Emma. Although she's naturally tired from her labours, she is so happy to have given birth to your son."

"Yes, all right, Alice, I am not myself at the minute anyway. I'll wash and change, and then maybe I'll feel a bit more sociable."

Having freshened up and changed his clothes James did feel physically better, but, he felt mentally drained. However, he made a determined effort to greet his wife with a smile. "How are you feeling now love?" he asked, taking her hand and kissing her gently.

"Is it all right if I bring the baby up for his feed now, Emma," called her mother from below stairs. "He must be disturbing you anyway."

"Nothing wrong with his lungs, James." said Emma with a smile. "Will you bring him up for his milk, or should I come down now."

"You stay where you are and get your strength back properly now. I'll go and get him," James answered.

When he returned with the baby James said, "Violet and Tom have just come home, and Alice has dinner ready for us. Will you be all right with the child while I go back down for my food?"

"Of course I will, my love," she answered with a smile. "My working man must be fed." Her reference to her 'working man' went through James heart like a knife, but he kept silent. When he reached the bottom of the stairs he saw that Thomas and Violet were sitting next to their grandmother, and both looked very anxious.

"James, I hope you don't mind me telling these two what happened today," said Edith. "They know not to say a word until their mother is up and about. Violet is going to have little Amy in with her tonight. So once you have all had dinner Alice and I will be off, but I will be back first thing tomorrow."

That night when James lay down beside her, Emma snuggled into him and laid her head on his chest. Holding her in his arms James was worried, knowing he would find it difficult to find work locally. There were just too many men out of work, and no jobs to be had. He knew this from a few of the unemployed men he had met in the Farmers Arms. One of them, John Morgan, had in desperation, gone to Brecon to sign up for the army.

The following day, Alice arrived in time for James to leave as if he were going to work. "Have you thought yet what is to be done about telling

Emma your bad news James?" she asked. "Although she won't be going out to see anybody for a few day's yet." she added. "I thought I would wait 'til the end of the week, or at least until she has got her strength back, Alice," he replied .

"Right you are James, and by then you may have better news of work."

"I'll be off now, see if there is any work about," he said. "Although I don't hold out much hope, not with things as they are."

That day James walked from one end of the town to the other in search of work. His efforts proved to be in vain. Three days went by, each the same as the last. James thought back to his childhood, when his father had reached an all-time low. Being unable to support his family had almost destroyed him. Memories of that terrible time prompted him to come to a difficult decision. He would join the army, but first, he would eat humble pie and go to see Lewis, Emma's father.

Lewis Davies and his wife Edith were at home together when James arrived. "Hello, James," said Edith, "What a surprise to see you this time of day. I hope there is nothing wrong. Are Emma and the baby all right?"

"Oh yes, they are both doing well," James replied swiftly. "I came to have a word with Lewis, and your good self."

Lewis looked up from his newspaper and with a slight frown. "I see, so sit yourself down and Edith will make us a hot drink."

"Would you like something to eat, James?" said his mother-in-law.

"No thanks, Edith," he replied. "I had breakfast before I came."

Edith returned with the tea before James spoke to them both of his dismissal. When asked why, by Lewis, he told them of his reaction to Tommy Davies' insulting remarks.

"I've heard a few tales about that damn chargehand and his methods, James," said Lewis thoughtfully. "And, under the circumstances, I can't blame you for having a go at him. So, financial help goes without saying, but what else can I do for you now?"

"Thanks for being so understanding, Lewis." James replied "I haven't stopped cursing myself since it happened, and I was expecting a right telling off from you." James paused, collecting his thoughts. "I have looked everywhere for work, there's just nothing available. The thought of being unable to take care of my family has driven me to a desperate decision. I intend to sign on for 'Queen's shilling' by joining up. Your generosity is greatly appreciated and I know you would never see Emma and the children without. The Queen's shilling is much less than the wages I've been earning. But without me to keep, it should be enough to keep the wolf from the door."

"I can sympathize with your way of thinking, James," said Lewis. "I'll be honest with you man, at first I was not too pleased about your marriage to my daughter. But you changed my mind for me. You're a good man, and I know Emma has never been happier. So, there's not just the money to think of. Does she know yet?"

"No she doesn't," James replied. "It's going to take all my courage to tell her and to stick to my guns, when she tries to dissuade me. Because I know that's what she will do. We had planned to go down to Llanboidy this weekend. Emma wants to show off our son to his other grandparents. So I will tell her when we get back."

Edith looked closely at James with tears in her eyes. "My girl will be devastated. She worships the ground you walk on, James. Won't you change your mind? Dear me, I am sure I don't know what to say."

"I think it best if we say no more, love," said Lewis to his wife. "We decided a long time ago that our children were old enough to make their own way in life. But you were right, James," he said turning to his son-in-law. "When you said we would never see Emma and the children without."

James returned home, relieved by the reactions of his in-laws.

As promised James took his family down to visit his parents that weekend. The whole family was delighted to welcome them and make a fuss over David Lewis and Amy.

Anne, who noticed that James was unusually quiet, asked him, "Are you all right, boy?"

"Yes, Mama I'm fine, but if you don't mind I would like to go and see Reverend Thomas before I go back. I won't stay long, I didn't get to see him last time I was home, and I felt a bit guilty after."

"For sure you go, and don't worry about us. I'll enjoy a good old chin wag with Emma. The children can play together, so we'll be fine," his mother replied.

The Reverend Thomas was busy preparing his sermon for Sunday service, when he saw James arriving. "James, this is a pleasant surprise."

"Hello, sir, I hope I'm not disturbing you?"

"Not at all, my boy, it's good to see you. I was just about to ask my kind housekeeper to make a pot of tea, will you join me James?"

"That sounds good to me, sir, I was hoping to have a talk with you." James looked serious as he spoke.

"Would you make tea for my visitor and I please, Mrs. Evans?"

"Yes indeed, Reverend," she answered. "I'll bring it in to you."

James waited until the housekeeper had brought the tea and left the room before he spoke. The good man listened carefully, as James told what had taken place at work and then of his plan to join the army. "You sound as if your mind is made up, James, so what is it that I can do to help?"

"The thing is this, sir," James hesitated. "I haven't told my wife or my parents yet, and I must be on my own with Emma when I tell her. And I can't do that here, so my problem is, I won't be able to tell my parents. I know my mother will be upset and that will let the cat out of the bag, so to speak."

"I understand your quandary, James, so do you want me to tell them when you have returned to Swansea?"

"That's very good of you, sir, but not exactly. I have written a letter which I hope you will give to them. This must seem very cowardly, but I don't think I could handle the reactions of both women, at the same time."

"I will do this for you boy, and in return I want you to do something for me." As he spoke the vicar handed James a leather bound Holy Bible and several writing books. "You must use these writing books as diaries, and keep a record of your life."

"Thank you, sir, I am grateful, but surely I will be doing this for myself — keeping a diary is supposed to be a private thing."

"So it is, James," said the vicar smiling. "However, it will give me much pleasure to know that your education is being put to good use." He paused, frowning. "I am afraid I am guilty of the sin of pride, when I think of the way you have mastered the art of copperplate writing. Always remember that copperplate writing is a very beautiful art. Use your gift well. That's settled, so enough from me, James. I must not keep you from your loved ones any longer."

James returned to find his mother, Emma and Aunt Martha laughing merrily. "There you are James," called his wife. "Your Aunt Martha has been telling me about your antics as a baby."

The rest of the day passed pleasantly for Emma, his mother, Martha and the numerous children. James was always gratified when his 'families' bonded.

Eventually it was time to leave. He hugged his mother tightly and as he shook his father's hand James desperately wanted to confide in him. Fear of the reaction by his mother and most of all his wife ensured his silence on the subject. Anne and Emma were occupied with hugs and goodbyes, when his father gave him a searching glance. *'He knows something is up,'* thought James. *'But there is nothing I do can do about it at this time.'*

When they arrived home everyone was tired. Violet and Thomas decided to go straight to bed. Emma needed to feed and change the baby, so James made them both a hot drink, before they also retired for the night.

The following day James decided to give one last effort to find work. It turned out to be fruitless, yet another heartbreaking day.

Emma was sitting in the big armchair nursing the baby when he arrived home, and little Amy was playing with her toys on the floor.

"James!" said his wife in surprise. "What are you doing home so early? You look awful, What is it ? What is wrong?"

"Emma, love, there is no nice way of telling you," he answered. "So I'll just come right out with it. I have lost my job. Your husband is out of work. And it was my own fault. Tommy Davies was out of order, and instead of taking it, I lost my temper and hit him."

He looked so desolate that her heart went out to him. "I'm so sorry my love, but don't take it so hard, you'll soon get another job, a big strong man like you. And we'll manage all right until you do. My father will help us out."

"My love," he said. "It happened days ago and I have tried, there is no work available. As for your father, I went to see him Tuesday. Like you say, he did offer to help out. But Emma, please try to understand, I can just about cope with him looking out for you and the children. There's no way I could live with him keeping me as well. So listen to me my dear, I have made up my mind to join the army."

"Oh no, James, I can't bear the thought of you leaving," cried a desolated Emma.

"I'm not leaving you, my love, it's only Brecon, I will be back at every chance I get." James took her into his arms as he fought back tears that threatened when he looked at her anguished face. "You are the love of my life. To leave you and our babes, is bad enough. I wish you could understand that this is something I have to do. Dry your tears now, my love. Put little David in his crib and give your pretty face a swill. I will comfort little Amy. She doesn't understand what's going on." He turned to his little girl saying, "Come to Dad, sweetheart, and have a cuddle."

Emma left them, as she dried her tears and made an effort to control her emotions. The arrival of Violet and Thomas from school, curtailed further conversation between James and Emma.

Later that evening when the three older children were asleep, a restrained Emma fed, and changed baby David. "Are you feeling better, Emma?" James asked, but without waiting for a reply he said, "Stay where you are love, I'm going to make us a cup of cocoa, Your mother gave me some of your father's brandy for you. To build up your strength, she said. I'll put a drop in your cocoa, it will also help you sleep. And then, my dear one, we will off to bed. We both need to get some rest."

"But James!" she exclaimed.

"No buts," he interrupted. "Off you go to bed, take baby David to his cot, and I'll bring the cocoa up."

James put a double measure of brandy into Emma's drink, hoping it would induce sleep. Once he was sure she was fast asleep he rose slowly, dressed and returned to the sitting room. He wrote a letter to Emma and a short note to Violet and one to Thomas. That done, he put four large potatoes in the oven to bake, before returning to the bedroom. He very quietly packed some clothing, without disturbing Emma. He placed the letter, notes and most of his wages on the dressing table. After a few hours of sleep on the big chair, James packed the potatoes together with some bread, cheese and a bottle he had filled with tap water. With heavy heart he left his home and family to begin his long walk to Brecon.

Walking along the Neath canal path in the darkness, James found it impossible to avoid the horse droppings. These were abundant, left by the horses which were used to pull barges. He took off his boots at the Briton Ferry crossing, cleaning them as best as he could with the cold water. Dawn was breaking as he walked through the neighbouring town of Neath. The freezing cold night air faded, becoming less severe. By his former calculations James assumed he had walked for more than twenty miles, and his legs and stomach told him it was time for a break. He stopped in front of a cemetery. There was a wooden bench just inside the entrance which seemed to appear just for him. He had no sooner sat down, when an old man and an old woman walked into the cemetery. The old woman walked on. But the old man stopped. He was well dressed and clean shaven, with mop of white hair. "Good morning to you, young man, my name is Albert Morris. I have been coming here every day for almost two years and this is the first time I have found company." His blue eyes twinkled as he smiled at James. "Do you also have a loved one buried here?"

"No sir, I don't," James replied. "I have just stopped for a rest, and something to eat."

"If you don't mind my company then we can eat together, and you can join me in a nice drop of hot tea." He opened his small carpet bag and took out a bottle filled with tea, and a pack of sandwiches. "I am in the habit of bringing some food and a drink to enjoy while I visit with my wife and two sons. They were taken with the cholera two years ago you see."

James expressed his sympathy for the man's loss. Then they talked amicably while James ate two of his potatoes followed by half of the bread and some cheese, which he washed down with a share of Albert's tea. "I was the local constable until my retirement fifteen years ago, which caused my dear wife many a sleepless night," Albert explained when he finished his food and drink. "However, there was very little crime in our village in those days. I'm afraid it's a different world we live in now. My gentle wife would be glad I had retired."

With thoughts of Emma's sadness once again invading his mind, James rose, shaking his head and body. After packing away the remainder of his food and drink he said goodbye to his new friend and continued his walk.

Midday was approaching as James caught his first sight of the of Brecon Beacons. He gazed at the vision of nature, exposed in her unadulterated state. The remote mountain ranges gave shade to the occasional evergreen bush of fern and golden brushwood. Half-hidden waterfalls escaped, making their way to wooded river valleys. For a brief moment his troubles were suppressed. He stared, fascinated, at the breathtaking beauty before him.

However, he was soon to realise that these rolling mountains held the most arduous test of his constitution. Nevertheless, he continued with fortitude, conquering the souring, craggy uplands, arriving at the peak as the sun was setting. He looked down and around, no longer able to appreciate the panoramic views, because he was almost exhausted. He decided to take a rest and eat the remainder of his food, before following the less taxing downward trek. Sunset approached as James finished the last of his food. Keeping some water for later he laid down under a large overhanging rock and slept until dawn broke.

Finally, he arrived at the Brecon Barracks on the morning of the eighth of December 1876. James attested under the name of his son, David Lewis. He used this alias so that he could abscond, if the need arose and avoid discovery by the powers that be.

CHAPTER 7
THE DIARY OF JAMES OWEN
ALIAS DAVID LEWIS

December 10th 1876.

There were half a dozen of us men signing on, or attesting as it's called, this morning. And a sorry looking lot we were, if not in stature, then definitely in appearance. This led me to thinking, that I am not the only desperate man looking for the Queen's shilling.

Later, we were in a line, getting our uniforms and clothing, when the funniest thing happened. There was suddenly the most awful smell! "Bloody hell who swallowed a rat?" shouted the soldier giving out the uniforms. We put our hands over our noses, and then we burst out laughing.

That is, all except one poor bloke who was blushing profusely. "Sorry boys," he said, with a shamefaced grimace, "But all I've had to eat for two days is the turnips I lifted from a field."

"Well bugger off out of here. Get to the mess as soon as you've dumped your gear," said the soldier.

Which I thought was a bit severe, even though the air still smelled foul. I met the other men, properly, while we were eating. All Welshmen, they were from in and around the Swansea valley. David Jones, a dark haired chap, is a little taller than me, but as thin as a rake(this was the man who had the wind problem). As it turns out he does have a naturally ruddy complexion, though it had been heightened earlier. He spoke little, maybe because he was concentrating on eating as much, and as fast as he could. Come to that we were, all six of us, tucking in.

David Morgan, the first thing you notice about him is his mop of thick dark ginger hair, which curls and waves from the top of his head down and covers his ears. That is the only thing about him that looks a little feminine. He is a very muscular looking man of medium height and build. His strong jaw is covered by a few days growth of ginger hair and his green eyes seem to look right through you. In fact, the intensity of his stare told me that he was sizing each of us up. Howard Davies — looks to be the healthiest and best kept of us. (I dread to think how I look at present). He appears to be about the same stamp as myself, maybe a little shorter. There the resemblance ends — his dark brown hair is streaked with grey, and his brown eyes give nothing away. He looks a lot older than the rest of us, may be in his late thirties, or more. David Llewellyn, I would say that this man will be a leader. Unremarkable in stature, he is of average height and weight, but with a handsome face, light brown hair and hazel eyes that seem to mirror intelligence. Also, he is well spoken, his accent is undeniably south welsh, melodious and easy on the ears. Gwynfor Rhys Jones — is another who is most unusual looking for a Welshman. He has pale skin, very light fair hair and pale blue eyes, reminding me of albinism, a pigment deficiency I have read about. He told us his appearance is inherited from his Danish mother.

While we were talking, a soldier approached us and greeting me like a long lost brother. I was nonplussed at first, although his face seemed familiar, I did not recognise him.

He explained that he was from my home village. His name is Hywel Griffiths, and he is a mate of my cousin Edward. Then I remembered his black hair, and dark skin, a fine looking chap, in spite of his large hooked nose. He used to work on the Graig Farm — a very grand farm, on a fabulous site, between the two tributaries of the Gronw river. When he addressed me as James Owen my heart sank. I had no choice but to come clean with my new friends. Fortunately we were not overheard, and present company agreed to keep my secret. There followed introductions all round, when David Llewellyn suggested we adopt 'nicknames. "I am quite accustomed to being called **Rick** due to my middle name being Richard," he said. "In a Welsh regiment there are sure to be many called David, we are four already, counting this 'David Lewis'. Gwyn and Howard should be all right as they are."

"Good thinking, Rick," replied David Morgan. "My mates all call me Morg, I prefer Morg to red, or ginger. And I suggest our friend David Jones, we call windy or gusty."

We all laughed at that, which was taken on the chin by our windy friend.

"You can all laugh, but I've been called worse. I'll settle for Gus if that suits you all."

"That leaves you David Lewis," Rick said, looking at me. "As we can't go into your past, I would suggest we call you Lewis.

"That will suit me fine," I replied. "Please be sure to remember this mate," I said to Hywel firmly. "Forget James Owen, I am now David Lewis, Lewis to my mates."

"Don't you worry about me, buddy boy, mum's the word on the subject. I am only sorry I never thought of doing the same," replied Hywel. We talked for a while before each one of us was glad to go and get some sleep. That evening began with strangers, who I felt, would become a firm band of good mates.

December 11th 1876.

All morning was spent on yard exercise and following marching orders. This afternoon we were taken by a corporal to a Quartermaster Sergeant who issued us with rifles called the Martini-Henry, with firm instructions that the remaining ammo was to be handed back straight after training. Instruction on the use and care of the rifles took place in a hall where all the new recruits were gathered. The sergeant in charge of this exercise went over and over again the importance of caring for the tool which would no doubt save or cost our lives. Later we were taken to a place called Slwch Trump, above Brecon, where rifle practice took place. These Martini-Henry rifles are fantastic. Just holding one makes a man feel invincible. It was a good day, cold but crisp and healthy feeling. Being outdoors, instead of in a stuffy warehouse, suits me fine.

Now that I am back in the barracks I am full of guilt again, thinking of my lovely Emma and the children.

December 18th 1876.

The past week has gone by so quickly. Drills, rifle practice, more drills and more rifle practice. The food and washing facilities are adequate, but some hot water to bath and shave would be so welcome. Gus has put on a some weight and is looking much healthier now. Gwyn has lost his paleness and his skin has taken on a more rugged appearance. When we are not tired out, we all feel much fitter men.

December 21st 1876.

I received a letter today from my dear wife. She is so angry at me for running off, and misses me badly, but she is coping all right and thankful for the money I am sending. The paymaster arranged a monthly remittance to be sent to Miss Emma Davies (for obvious reasons I gave her maiden name). Although we are paid the Queen's shilling, half is taken out for keep, laundry and so on. She addressed the letter as she was told to Private David Lewis, but she started with, My dear instead of Dear David. I guess she can't get around to calling me David. Life here doesn't change, one day folds into another. Apart from my letter there is nothing new to write in this diary.

December 23rd 1876.

We were told yesterday that we have a three day furlough for Christmas! Hywel has a lift for us tomorrow morning, with a friend who delivers goods to Brecon. He has promised to drop me off in Swansea on his way to Llanboidy. I have made some extra money writing letters and Christmas cards, for some of the boys who can't write. So I will go into the village this afternoon to see if I can get some gifts for the family.

December 27th 1876.

This was the best and the worst Christmas I have ever spent. Being with my lovely wife and children was the best. I held my little one and played games with the children. Emma and I made love all night on my first night home, and again on the night before I left. We had a grand Christmas day. Emma's mother, father and Alice came for the day. We feasted on roast chicken and vegetables followed by Christmas pudding and custard. Emma's father brought wine to have with dinner and then port for after.

Leaving them was the worst. I sneaked away again in the early hours of the morning. I had previously arranged to meet Hywel at the end of the road, knowing I would want to avoid impossible goodbyes once more.

January 18th 1877.

We were told today that we are to be posted to the 2nd battalion 24th Regiment of Foot which is based at Dover Citadel. There is a hive of activity in every part of the barracks. The move is to take place on the twenty-second of the month. This leaves a minimum amount of time for preparations to be made. I have written to my Emma, I hope the news will not upset her too much.

February 23rd 1877.

The barracks here in Dover are just another barracks, nothing to write home about. Me and the boys have settled in all right and are making the best of things. We have been to the local inn a couple of times to drown our sorrows as we did in Brecon. Other than that life here follows the same pattern.

July 24th 1877.

There has been very little to write about for the last few months. My life in this man's army has been made bearable only because of my good mates and because I am able to send money home. Rick keeps telling us that that this is 'the calm before the storm' so we should make the most of it and stop moaning.

November 11th 1877.

We are being posted to the main battalion, 24th of Foot, who are stationed in Chatham. Gwyn told us that his older brother, who is also with the 24th, was moved there in June. Word has it that an extended army is being mustered to join in the African war. So it seems that we are to be prepared for a big shove.

January 31st 1878.

Chatham is a much bigger military base than the others we were in. There is a large contingent of the 2nd battalion of the 24th regiment here, and more officers than I have seen before, in one place. The last two months have been hectic. Drills and target practice from morning to night. We are to leave for Portsmouth on the third of February, where we will board ship for Africa.

February 5th 1878.

Two days ago we came to Portsmouth by troop train which was packed to the rafters, with well over one thousand men. It wasn't too bad though — the crazy jokes and banter with the boys helped to pass the time. Still, we were glad to get off the train and board ship.

The Himalaya is a 3,438 ton coal-fuelled troop ship. Considering I was told she had been the largest passenger ship in the famous P&O Fleet, she offers very little in the way of comfort. Our sleeping quarters are in the bows of the ship and packed tightly together. The meager space between hammocks is just enough to place a pair of legs and feet.

We had barely set sail when men began spewing, and not all of them reaching the decks let alone the rails. I think I must be a good sailor, because as yet, I haven't felt any ill effects.

At first I found the noise of the ship's propeller drove me crazy when I was trying to sleep. But I am getting used to it and not letting it bother me as much. The rocking of the ship was making it difficult for me to write clearly, but I am also getting used to that.

February 10th 1878.
Conditions aboard are becoming worse. More and more men are going down with sickness and diarrhoea. The hardened sailors are all fine so are many of us who have never sailed before. Teams of us are on constant cleaning up duty, washing down the decks and cleaning up below. Below is the worst because of the stench. Even those of us who have remained healthy want to throw up and some do. We have to clean around the poor devils who can't move off their beds, and they smell foul. 'I'd

rather be dead' is the cry we often hear from them. And I think some of them soon will be, they look so ill. We are worried about Gwyn, he is looking rough. The rest of my mates are all right so far.

February 14th 1878.

I was woken up this morning by Rick. He was shaking my shoulders saying, "Wake up, Lewis for God's sake. Gwyn is in hell of a state, I think his number's up. Come on, we can't let those bloody body baggers get to him first."

I moved as fast as I could, pulling on my trousers, vest and boots as I went. When we got to Gwyn he was lying across his bed with his head hanging over the side. His face was a horrible shade of grey, and he was shaking and retching. Evil looking green bile spouted from his mouth and through his nose.

"Oh my God, Gwyn boy, come on up. Take hold of his other arm mate," I asked Rick. "And we'll see if we can get him comfortable. Then we must try to get some fluids into him."

Doing as I asked, Rick said, "Right then, I haven't drunk all my ration of rum so I'll go and get it for him."

"Good God, no man," I replied. "Don't you know that liquor dries you out? What he needs is plenty of good water. See if you can filch some."

When Rick had gone, the boys on cleaning up duty came and they cleaned around Gwyn first. They loaned me a wet cloth, so I cleaned up his face and neck.

"Is it you, Lewis?" he whispered.

"Yes, mate I'm here to stay, and good old Rick has gone for some water for you," I said, trying to keep the panic out of my voice.

"I think I'm done for, my friend. Goodbye, James Owen." With my real name on his lips Gwyn passed away. Rick hurried back with the water, but he was just too late to say goodbye to our friend. We sat alongside Gwyn, until the body baggers came. By this time Morg, Gus and Howard had joined us. Between us we wrapped our mate's body, so that the body baggers didn't have to manhandle him. Rick, Howard, Gus, Morg, Hywel, me, and a few others that we had got to know, watched him being buried at sea this afternoon. Three other poor boys went the same way. I said one of the prayers that the Reverend Thomas said at funerals and the boys joined in with the amen.

March 6th 1878.

At last I have some good news to write about! Land was sighted this morning. It is hoped that we will arrive in about two or three days in East London. Cheers went out from men at intervals as they heard the news. Most of the worst sickness stopped a week ago and we haven't had a death for days. So we are hoping that those who are still quite week, will have regained most of their strength. And so we will still have a formidable military force to join the rest of the army. If only poor Gwyn could be with us to celebrate.

March 12th 1878.
Today the Himalaya anchored a couple of miles from shore. She was unable to get closer because the reefs were impossible to negotiate. B and C company were the first to be set ashore in surf boats. Fortunately, I and my mates were amongst the first, but it was pouring with rain and we were soaked through to our skin. By the end of the first day, I was told that more than eight hundred men were landed. And the remainder would take another day or more to land.

We were brought by train to our barracks in King William's Town. Waiting in line for our turn to board the train, and then the journey in our wet clothes was most uncomfortable. This place seems more like a different world rather that another country. The land behind the town consists of mountains, deep ravines and rocky bush. The military base is a large camp site situated outside the town. There are a few buildings — the ammunitions depot, the hospital, and the cookhouse. There are several wagons around a corral in which huge oxen are kept. Rick, Gus, Howard, Morg and me were brought into a large bell-shaped tent with about twelve others. We mates managed to occupy a corner of the tent where we could bunk down next to each other. Hywel and his mates Charlie Evans and Billy Hopkins are bunked next to us.

March 12th 1878.

My part in this war has begun. We have been fighting for the past two days, against a Kaffir tribe called the Gealekas who live on the other side of the river. The river is called the Great Kei and the territory on this side, has, for some time been named the British Kaffraria. The Kaffir tribe who live on this side of the river are called the Gaika, These Kaffirs are on our side against the Gealeka, because they have been at war some time, over territory

Gealeka Kaffirs use the bush as cover and they throw their assegais. These are short shafted spears with a wide blade, and are used as a sword or a spear. They also have a type of club that they use to beat a man's brains out. And some of them have rifles, with which they take pot shots at us.

March 14th 1878.

Skirmishes have taken place every day. For us mates, today was different. We were ordered to form a line, then to penetrate the bush and flush the kaffirs out, towards the waiting troops. The areas of shrub are so thick that a man can't see more than a few feet in front of him, so a kaffir can be on him without warning. This type of skirmish isn't what we expected of warring! The Martini-Henry in the bush is used as a bayonet rather than as a rifle. The first time we went in, we came out within minutes because we just could not negotiate the bush. But we were sent back in! The second time, we did manage to flush out several Kaffirs. They were disposed of by the waiting riflemen. Rick and me emerged almost together, followed by Howard, Gus, Morg and then the rest of our line. But Danny, from our tent, was missing. I looked at Rick and, without a word, we both headed back into the bush to find him. We soon found him, his head had been beaten to a pulp. His boots and his rifle had been taken and his coat was half off. We finished removing his coat and wrapped it around his poor head. We carried him out and brought his body back to camp.

Danny's terrible death hit us badly but most of all, it disturbed Howard. He broke down when he saw the state of poor Danny's body. It was terrible to see a grown man cry and then swearing about this god-forsaken country. Gus took him aside and spoke quietly; we still don't know what he said but it worked. Howard walked quietly back with him to the camp, while me and Rick carried Danny's body.

March 15th 1878.
Today was a little easier. The five of us were on rifle duty, on the perimeter of the bush. We are all good shots and made out targets, and Howard did as well as the rest of us. Gus went with Howard to see the surgeon this morning. He gave Howard a type of powder to dissolve in water. It must have done the trick, because our friend looks to be back in shape.

March 28th 1878.
A surprising letter came for today from my good friend, big Dai. But it is dated the eighteenth of December, 1876! It was originally posted to Brecon, so I can see why this one took so long to get to me. Dai has put on the envelope, 'Brecon Town', instead of 'Brecon Barracks'. It must have 'gone around the mulberry bush' before it got to me. I think I am lucky to get it. He writes to tell me about Tommy Davies getting a violent beating by a person or persons unknown, on the night I left for

Brecon! Dai is of the opinion that no one is surprised. Because too many enemies have been made by that treacherous sod, including all the mates of James Owen! And there is more than one who will not be sorry to see him carried out in a wooden box. Which the boys have been told is quite likely. He also says that the law men have been asking questions about me. The police were told that I had a fight with Tommy, and that I bore a grudge. Dai and my mates from work were questioned and each one had to go to Mr Lloyd's office, where they were grilled by an officer of the law. They gave nothing away, saying the fight between me and Tommy meant nothing. Since then, they have tried to find the snitch, but without any luck. Edward told them that Emma hasn't been bothered so the law must be satisfied by the boy's explanations. But the thing is, if Tommy dies it will be murder. So who knows what more is to come. But, he tells me not to worry! Other news from home he writes is that he sees Emma and my family daily. His wife shops and keeps company with her when the children are at school. All are well and baby David is thriving and already ruling the roost! I am told again, not to worry about them.

Edward has been made temporary chargehand while Tommy is off sick. So, even though everybody still works hard, the boys are finding that working conditions are so much better. Also, the atmosphere has changed dramatically, for the better. The boys still go down to the Farmers Arms on Friday evenings for a few drinks. Big Dai's son Bobby asked to pass on his best regards and his wife also sends her best regards.

April 12th 1878.
The daily skirmishes we are sent out on seem to be getting less vicious. The Kaffirs are hiding deeper into the bush, where our men have learnt not to follow. There have been fewer injuries and no fatalities for days.

April 20th 1878.
News has it that we are winning! The tribal chief of the Gealeka called Kreli was killed, and we dispatched most of his force, the Kaffirs who live this side of the river. The Gaikas, are rejoicing with us because of their hatred of the Gealeka as their sworn enemies.

April 29th 1878.
The boys and I had a trip into town yesterday. We had a few drinks at an inn where there was a group of the 1st 24th gathered. I'm not sure how it started, but a rumpus broke out. I was at the bar with Rick and Howard when we looked toward the noise.

Morg, who is easily identified, was in the middle of a fine brawl, and he was seriously out numbered. "Come on boys," said Rick, but, we were already on the move. Then I saw young Charlie Evans, and his mate Billy Hopkins, who were rushing from the other side of the room. They had seen what was happening, and were also going to help Morg. What a shindy we had! The bartender broke it up with a gunshot, and the threat of calling the military police.

I think that the boys from the first will have second thoughts before they tangle with us again. We more than held our own against odds of better than two to one. Morg told us later that a fellow from the first made sport of his red hair, which caused an outbreak out of laughter? "Well, boys," he said, "I'd had just about enough from that lot. They think they are better than us just because they have been here longer. I landed a beauty on the mouthy one and I think I broke his nose. I heard a crack before he yelled." He grinned before he went on, "Now I really look a sight, with a black and blue face to contrast with my red hair." We all laughed with him. As a result we all had more to drink, and ended up singing our way back. We were staggering towards the barracks, when we saw a couple of the first sergeants. They were coming towards us from the opposite direction.

"Run boys, before they see us in this state," I said taking off as fast as I could. We all got back, including Charlie and his mate, to our tent, within minutes of each other, except for Howard — he had not made it.

"Wasn't Howard behind with you, Gus?" asked Rick.

"Well he was," replied Gus "I thought he just fell back a bit. I didn't miss him until I was nearly here. And then it was too late. I hope he wasn't caught in that state."

"We are all in the same state," said Rick. There is nothing we can do to help Howard tonight. If we go out looking for him we are just going to draw the wrong attention and make things worse. Just hit the sack, and if anyone comes looking, pretend to be asleep. If Howard walks in now, he'd better not disturb me."

The following morning I awoke to find Howard's bed had not been slept in! Rick and Gus were both stirring at the same time.

"Oh my God," said Gus. "Where's Howard? What could have happened to him?"

"Will you wake up that lazy sod next to you?" I asked Gus "We need to talk."

Gus shook Morg, none too gently, saying, "Wake up, Morg, we got big trouble."

"What's up?" said a surprised Morg. "What's going on?"

"Be quiet, we don't want to be over heard. Howard didn't get back last night," said Rick keeping his voice down. He's either fallen in a drunken sleep somewhere, or he's been arrested. I hope to God it's the former."

"You're probably right, Rick," I said. "So let's move ourselves and hope we find him first, and before reveille."

We searched the entire camp, until it was time for morning parade, but found no sign of Howard. During roll call the sergeant passed Howard's number — it was as if he knew there would be no answer. Gus approached the sergeant later and asked after Howard. He was told that Howard was in hospital! The hospital was at the other end of the camp, a good five or six minutes from where we were standing. I think we made it in two.

His own mother would not have recognized him! His face had been battered to a pulp. "Jesus, Howard what has happened to you?" asked a very shocked Rick. He tried to talk, but his lips were so swollen that only strange laboured sounds came out. "Forget it, mate," I said. "Time enough to tell the tale when you get better. For now just concentrate on getting strong and well. If there is anything you need, or anything we can do, try to find a way of letting us know."

"Can you write, Howard, if we bring you in paper and pen?" asked Rick.

In reply Howard brought his hands painfully out of the covers. His right hand was bandaged the other had bruises and the start of scabbing at the knuckles.

May 2nd 1878.

There has been gradual improvement in Howard's condition. He is at least able to talk to us. But he still has so much pain from his tightly bandaged ribs which were broken, and bad headaches, which I don't like the sound of. Today he was able to tell us what had happened to him. The sergeants had been with the Firsts at the inn, they were also very drunk. They caught him and laid into him. "As you know boys, if we had been caught, the punishments dished out for drunks is terrible," Howard told us. "I felt I was on a hiding to nothing, so I got stuck in, and fought back. They didn't get it all their own way."

May 11th 1878.

When Rick and I arrived at the hospital today we saw a couple of sergeants leaving. Howard told us that they had been to see him!

"One of them did all the talking, the Irish one," said Howard. "He said, they wanted me to know that they did not intend the beating to go so far. They had both been drinking and were looking for a fight." Howard paused and pointed to a bunch of fruit. "They also brought me these oranges and lemons, so they can't be that bad can they?"

"Good God, Howard boy, this must be a first!" replied Rick. "The hard cases in this army don't ever show a soft side."

"I don't know so much Rick," I said. "They, particularly one of them, are probably decent blokes, when they are home. Out here, living in these vile conditions, is enough to drive any man over the edge. It's Howard's decision though. Do we go for them, as planned, or should we let sleeping dogs lie?"

"Forget about any retribution please, boys," replied Howard. "I don't want any more trouble, not for me or for you."

May 29th 1878.

Today the regiment gave a funeral for the Kaffir chief, Sandilli, of the friendly Gaikas. It was a very posh affair. The Kaffirs wore their best finery, grand head ornaments and all sorts of gear made of feathers and beads. The battalion turned out in full uniform. And I, together with Gus, two corporals and two sergeants, were among the pall-bearers! Word has it that we are soon to join the regiments in the Natal where the war against the Zulu tribes is raging. My worry is, that Howard could get left behind if he is unfit.

CHAPTER 8
THE DIARY PART TWO

June 1ˢᵗ 1878.

Great news, at least we think it's good. Howard has been discharged from hospital as fit! He is very glad to be back with us, so I suppose we must be happy for him. Even though, I for one have my doubts about his fitness for the journey we have ahead! Extra wagons have arrived with more oxen and mules, to pull all the stores, ammunition and tents. I have been on packing and loading duty since early afternoon — thankfully the weather has been kind, and we stopped at about six-thirty. Tomorrow, I am due for lookout duty. Am I glad! All this hauling heavy loads is hard on the back.

September 14ᵗʰ 1878.

The past few months have been hard labour. When we set off the noise was incredible. Drivers cracked their whips which sounded like gun shots. The oxen bellowed and the wheels of the wagons screeched. Officers mounted on neighing horses and foot soldiers marched with hearty voices. I don't who started singing. It must have been a Welshman, because the strains of Men of Harlech floated into my ears. The rest of the Welsh soldiers, to man, joined him. I sang along with them pushing down a lump in my throat. Looking around, I saw that there were men, hardened soldiers, with tears in their eyes!

Such a column had been slow to move over difficult terrain. The great oxen stumbled over potholes, wheels came off wagons and men were caught beneath falling oxen and debris. The blistering hot weather made everything dry and dusty, which caused dry, sore eyes and coughing. At night we slept where we dropped. Rick and I usually managed to get a place for Howard, and sometimes the rest of our mates, beneath a wagon. Torrential downpours came without warning and just as suddenly stopped. This meant that we were often sleeping in wet clothes, on hard ground. On the march our clothes would dry out in the intense heat, and steam rose from the men's clothing, and from the animals' coats.

We have come about seventy-four miles, from King William's Town to Pietersmaritzburg, where we have a reasonably comfortable camp, which, after that horrific journey, seems grand. But, there have been more deaths, mainly those who were very low while travelling.

September 18th 1878.

Most of our boys, including me, have recovered physically. Howard is still not the man he was, but he is so much better since we have been here.

I was talking this morning to David Rhys, a young lad who is in our tent. He was sentenced to twenty-five lashes for falling asleep at his post, but then his sentence was remitted. He is hoping it will be forgotten — if not, then at least he is stronger now to deal with it. I told him not to worry, that they would want us all in good shape to go up against the Zulus. I hope I was right! I must be even more cautious with my use of paper. I had to remove two pages of this diary for paper on which to write home. The price of one sheet of paper can be as much as one shilling!

The news that we are to push on soon, towards Zululand, has caused much unrest among the men — several soldiers, and many of the Kaffirs, have deserted.

January 1879.

Yet again we have marched mile upon mile, through this godforsaken land and now we are in Zulu territory. The last lap was over the river called the Buffalo to a mission station called Rorke's Drift. The entire company, including over four thousand men, wagons oxen and stores, were brought over in pontoons. Our warring now is against a different breed of Kaffir. The Zulus are no hordes of poorly organized rabble to be dismissed lightly. We've been informed that the column is to move out of Rorke's Drift on Friday January the twelfth (tomorrow) without us! "B" Company of the second Battalion of the 24th (that's us all right), have been assigned as a permanent garrison, to guard the Drift.

This news has been met with various reactions from the men of our company. Some are disappointed, some are downright depressed, but most of us are just hopping mad. The fault was immediately laid at the lieutenant's door. To a man we agreed on the assumption that he had assented to a request that he had not even heard. Because as usual he was trying to hide the fact that he is as deaf as a post! I don't doubt that what we are all thinking is true, but I can't help feeling sorry for him today. He's never shown a lack of courage and he's always been more than fair with us men. The poor sod can't help going deaf and I for one don't blame him for trying to hide it. No man with his rank and prospects would risk being pensioned off at thirty odd.

Since the news broke; there has been feverish activity all over the camp. My lot have been put on duty fortifying the station, which will take several days.

January 12th 1879.

The main column moved out this morning. Within about half an hour we heard rifle shooting and the sounds of firing. The sergeant major told us that the enemy had been engaged and dispatched, so our boys got safely through to Isandlwana.

January 18th 1879.

Late yesterday morning a rich trader with another driver arrived from Greytown, leading two wagons. Each wagon was full to busting with gin, tobacco and cigars. Howard, Morg, Gus and me were amongst the last to buy from him. We had been occupied for best part of the morning, writing last minute letters for the boys who can't read or write.

Although our writing hands ached we were well pleased because our pockets jingled with the money we had earned. We never take money from our own boys mind you, but all others we charge a ha'penny a letter, and they provide their own paper. We bought enough gin to 'drown our sorrows' and more than enough baccy, to hand some around in the mess. When we were walking away from the wagons Gus had a thunderbolt idea! "There seems to be an awful lot of gin and baccy left on those wagons, boys," he said thoughtfully. "It would be a pity for that bloke to have to cart it all back to Greytown." He paused giving each one of us a searching look. "Especially as we, and our boys, are going to be stuck in this godforsaken hole for who knows how long." He continued. "In dire need of the occasional consolation we'll be, won't we now? Everybody knows that the half gill a day ration of gin they give us, well, that hardly wets the whistle, now does it?" Howard, Morg and I just looked at each other and then back to Gus incredulously, each of us realising immediately the full implications of his words. I grinned and my head shook, but Howard started to protest wildly. He was soon silenced by a finger to the mouth gesture from me and a quiet, but firm request from Gus to 'hold his horses' 'til we're back at our tent.'

We walked the rest of the way in silence, each of us deep in our own thoughts. By the time we got back to the tent it was five p.m. It had already begun to get dark and we could feel the cold night air starting its journey through our flesh. Gus being last in started to secure the tent flap down. Before he had chance to finish his task, Howard started to spout nervous gibberish, about being tied to wagons, lashings, the firing squad and God knows what unbelievable punishments would be handed out to us. At the same time Gus was telling him to 'shut up a minute, give it a rest for God's sake', and more. At last there was a breathing space, which I took immediate advantage of. "Howard," I said putting my hand on his shoulder. "None of this night's events can affect you anyway as you have got an evening watch. You and Charlie are due to relieve Rick and Billy, shortly on the Oskarburg aren't you?"

Howard looked at me vacantly, momentarily struck dumb, then he nodded. Gus began to laugh, saying, "That'll make history that will. I bet that's the first time anybody's forgotten a bloody Oskarburg watch, never mind being glad they've got one."

We all grinned at this and then Howard said sheepishly, "Look, boys, I'm thinking of you as well you know. There's enough trouble already without looking for it. We've already lost poor old Gwyn to dysentery and Danny to a murdering Kaffir. At least their families will be told that they died in the line of duty. Think of what can happen if you're caught, please." He was looking anxiously at me. I knew he was thinking of how he suffered in Kings Williams Town.

"Right boys, I don't know about you but I'm ready for something to eat." I said truthfully, but I also wanted to stop that particular conversation. "Come on, let's go for food, before the ditch gets all the grub that's left."

Gus was quick to get my drift. "Good thinking, 'cos there will be more than one measly gill of gin going down us tonight." He laughed and slapped his stomach. Howard heaved a sigh of relief, he fooled himself into thinking that the crazy idea of looting the good wagons had been shelved. As I started out with Gus and Morg, Howard began to follow us but he stopped, saying, "Aren't we going to take some of our gin and baccy to hand out in the mess?"

Turning my head but not stopping, I said, "You do that, Howard, there are sure to be some poor buggers who had no money. I've got a full bottle of fin so you can sort out some baccy and follow us down."

When we were out of earshot, Gus said to me, "Well, what do you think, Lewis? We can't rush in like a bull at a gate, but it will have to be done tonight. Have we got enough time to make a plan and go for it?"

"Too right we do," I replied. "If I hadn't been so busy thinking about the money I can send home from the writing, I would have been having the exact same thoughts as you. And I'm damn sure the same will go for Rick." We continued to walk while we talked, so that we stayed well ahead of Howard. "Once we've had our food we'll fill a plate to take back to the tent for Rick. That way we can talk while he's eating and waste no time in getting ourselves organised. Howard will be out of the way because he is on guard duty at the other end of the Oscarburg." By this time we had reached the mess tent. "That's it for now, boys," I said quietly. "No more talk until we're on our own back in our tent."

When Gus, Morg and I got back to our tent at was dark and the camp was quiet. We guessed we had an hour or two before everybody, with the exception those on guard duty, would be asleep. We were sitting on my sleeping bag going over the plan we had worked out, when Rick came hurrying into the tent, stooping to enter. "Jammy sod I am, boys," he said. "I made it back just as it's starting to rain again. Bad enough up there in the cold," he said, looking at in the direction of the Oscarburg. "Without having the rain an' all. Howard will have it rough, poor bugger. By the time the rain stops he'll be soaked and freezing, But then, he said he's going to risk a smoke or two in one of the caves where he won't be spotted. And he'll warm himself up with a drop of gin now and then." He had removed his topcoat while he was talking and then Gus took it from him saying, "Belt up for a minute will you, we have got something to tell you, so get this down you and listen while you're eating. Now sit there," he said pointing to the big trunk and passing Rick his food. Gus told him of our plan, after briefing him on the events of the afternoon. I enjoyed watching his reactions, his eyes widening when he was told what remained in the goods wagons, and then narrowing thoughtfully when he knew what we meant to do.

He looked from one to the other and quite calmly he said, "Well now, if I am going to get cold and wet after all, boys, I want to be pretty sure I dry off, with a nice drop of gin. So let's hear how we are to go about this business, without getting caught and tied to a bloody wagon wheel or worse."

This was my cue. I showed Rick the rough sketch I had made of the route we would take, to and from the goods wagons. Pointing with my pencil I explained, "This is our tent third from last, now then we move quietly to the end of the tents line and then using our noses we turn right, away from the stinking ditch. We then run like hell the fifty yards or so down the bank to the cookhouse. Once there me and Rick go in and to pick up one of the big containers with a lid. We needn't worry about being quiet then, the din from those bloody frogs will drown any noise we could make.

"Then, it's easy does it, round the back of the hospital, to the far end of the kraal, where the goods wagons are pitched. Gus will keep watch, well he will listen anyway for anybody coming, while we fill the container and sacks. Coming back will be harder work 'cos we'll have the load to carry. Are you with me?"

"I'm with you all right, but what I want to know is what the hell do we want with a heavy container?" said Rick.

"That's where Gus comes in," I replied. "That part is his brilliant idea, so I'll let him tell you himself."

"Well, I thought of it when we were working out where to hide the stuff afterwards," said Gus with a grin. "There are loads of good places up on the Oskarburg that we can dig. The gin can go in the sacks, but, we've got to keep some of the stuff dry 'specially the baccy. So, what better than a strong container with a lid, to keep it all nice and protected?"

"What about Howard," said Rick. "Is he in on this crazy scheme?"

"No," I replied. "I don't think Howard has got over the last time, when he got caught after we had that bust up, with some of the Firsts, in King William's Town. I can tell you boys, he paid hard for that night's entertainment. Anyway, he's just not up to it any more so it's just the four of us, and no grudges about Howard mind, we don't really need him."

They each nodded their agreement and then the four of us got down to perfecting our plans.

Two hours later, after waiting for the heavy rain to subside a little, we set out. Everything went according to plan until we were just about to round the corner of the hospital. We came to a sharp halt when we heard voices coming from the front veranda to our left. We couldn't make out what they were saying, but we easily identified the melodious Irish tones of the surgeon and the low rumblings of the reverend. The voices stopped, so I took a chance and peaked around the corner. I could just make out the broad back of the surgeon and towering above him the outline of a man, in a flowing robe, which had to be the reverend. They stood in the dim light, which came through the open door. Then I froze and broke out into a cold sweat! The Reverend Smith was looking right at me! His thick red beard glowed as it caught the light and his dark piercing eyes bored into my brain. Then he raised his hand, grunted what must have been good night to the surgeon, and he just started to walk away!

I had, for a moment, forgotten that he was standing in the light, and I was hidden in the darkness. I watched him walk towards the mission, his old, mildewed looking church frock hanging wet about his enormous feet. I breathed a sigh of relief when his tall form faded into the darkness. Surely that was the last we would see of him this night. We continued around the kraal to the goods wagons, the darkness of the night and the noise from the frogs helped but also hindered. They made sure we were not seen or heard but they prevented us from seeing or hearing also. Therefore, we progressed slowly, stopping and listening every few yards until we reached the back of the wagons. Then we stopped again. We guessed that the man and his other driver would be asleep in a wagon, but we were not sure if they would be in the same one. Rick and I stayed put while Gus took a look around the wagons and back. He pointed to the first wagon, just below us. "They're both in this one, drunk as lords and snoring like the devil," he whispered when he returned, "So get going."

Rick climbed into the second wagon and checked the contents. "All in here boys so pass up the container, Morg," he said. "You go to the other end, Lewis and fill the sacks." Once in the wagon I lost no time, putting as many bottles of gin as I could, into the sacks, and then passed them down to Gus who was waiting below. I took one of the sacks and Gus carried the other. Rick and Morg took hold of the container, a side handle each. It was heavy, but with both of them carrying, it was no worse full than empty. They said thanks that cigars and baccy don't weigh much. We made our way up towards the Oskarburgh. Once we had passed safely through the camp the tension began to lift. When we reached the spot that Gus had decided on, Rick and Morg dropped the container, we took the sacks off our backs and we sank to the ground. "Is this the perfect hiding spot you told us about Gus?" asked Rick. "Why it's one of the first places they'll look man!"

"Oh no it's not then," replied Gus, reaching behind a small boulder and producing a shovel. "I remembered leaving this shovel here last Thursday. Do you know what this is then?" he said pointing to a large mound of earth. It was pretty dark still so we could only just make it out. "This is where the bloody Kaffir lays, that me and the diggers buried last week."

"Jesus, boy," said Rick. "You don't mean we're putting loot in with a dead body, do you?"

"What better place is there?" I asked. "They won't think he's hiding our stuff. Nope, nobody's going to want to look down there. And after the hullabaloo dies down we'll move it into one of the caves up here. Once they've searched all the likely places it will be safe to move, but we'll wait a few days and move it for storing."

The earth was soft and recently dug over which made Gus's task quick and easy. Rick and Morg lifted the body sack out, put down the container with the gin sacks alongside. We replaced about half of the earth, enough to cover the loot and then we laid the body over the top. We shoveled the remaining earth back replacing it all carefully, leaving no sign of disruption. "Wait a minute," whispered Gus. "I can smell smoke boys, Howard must be nearby." Putting my hand to my mouth in order to silence Gus, I took a deep breath. Sure enough there it was, blowing towards us from above. Pointing upwards, I then beckoned the boys to follow me, quietly.

We made it back without any more bother, although our heavy topcoats were thoroughly drenched by this time. And we were shivering. "Bloody hell, boys, and to think we were grumbling about the heat not so long ago," Gus moaned, as we all removed the offending clothes and boots.

"Aye," said Rick. "Well let's have a bit of hush now and get some sleep." I lay down wondering if I would be able to sleep that night, but I must have dosed off, because the next thing I remember is hearing the sound of reveille.

January 19th 1879.

Gus woke with a weary groan and a few muttered moans while me and Rick concentrated on getting ready for parade. "All hell has been let loose boys," said Howard bursting into the tent. " I came hotfoot down when I heard reveille start, but when I got to the first tent row Corporal Williams stopped me. He told me to get back to my post 'cos reveille was an hour early, due to a big search for stolen goods. I haven't got time to hang about, but I had to warn you."

"You get back, Howard boy. Thanks for the thought but you needn't have worried about us. Some other bugger must have had the same idea as Gus. You must admit it was very tempting." Rick lied convincingly, and I hoped I looked calmer than I felt. Howard grinned widely and with a " Yes, I believe that, thousands wouldn't." Then he made a quick exit.

"Come on then, boys, not too eager mind or someone will smell a rat. Let's just go our normal stride like innocent little lambs," said Rick, making an effort to be jovial. "Bloody hell, my boots and coat are still soaking wet."

"Yes, well that's very uncomfortable for you, boyoh, and another problem for us. You can say they didn't dry out after your watch, but how are we going to explain our wet clothes, Lewis?" Morg asked looking at me with a worried frown.

"We don't have to," I replied, after a minutes thought. "It's still drizzling a bit so we'll put them on get to the end of the furthest line and hope we're amongst the last to be searched. By that time we'd have been soaked anyway." Looking from one to the other I continued. "Now for God's sake dress tidy today, we don't want to draw attention to ourselves by being called out of line." They nodded and continued to dress, still hurrying but with more care. We made our way to the lines listening all the while to the comments of the other men. If we weren't so damned apprehensive we would have roared with laughter. Particularly when from one small group we heard someone call the event 'a bloody great caper, that he would love to have been in on'. Once in line we became oblivious to the discomfort of our cold wet clothes and thanked God that the rain continued to fall. We were also fortunate that Corporal Harris inspected our line — he was never as keen as the command sergeant major, and today he was obviously less than happy with his duty, so we found ourselves hastily searched, dismissed and sent on our way back to quarters. We were not surprised to find our tent in messed up by the search party, because we had heard the grumblings and cursing of men in the tents we had passed for the same reason. However, we were so relieved to be back without detection that we readily took off our coats and tidied up the tent in no time at all. I can't remember who started the laughing, It was either Rick or Morg, but I couldn't help joining in. "We did it! We bloody well did it!" cried Morg through his laughter.

January 22nd 1879.

This was a terrible day, one that will haunt my comrades, and me, as long as we live. Early that afternoon, two or three men came from Isandlwana. They said that the main camp had been attacked. All twelve hundred or more men had been slaughtered by a huge Zulu army of four thousand or more! They thought that only they had escaped. And they came to warn us that the Zulus were coming for Rorke's Drift, thousands of them! The orders came out to fortify the camp. Rick and I were sent to join the men who had already begun to move sacks of corn and produce to form blockades. We made a line and passed the sacks along, building a mealy bag wall, beginning at the front of the hospital to join up with the stone kraal wall.

Howard, Gus and Morg were with a larger group. They were moving a couple of wagons from the corral to the back of the hospital, up to the commie stores. Biscuit tins were used to form a protective barrier across the open parade ground. Our rows of tents were swiftly taken down, so that we had a clear view of an attack if it came towards the commie. stores. The cooks were ordered to put out all fires. I remember hoping they would have some way of keeping hot soup for us. When I think back, what a stupid thought at such a time! We had barely formed our defences before they came. We heard the noises first, of hundreds of hardened bare feet running towards us, followed by the beating of spears against shields. Every soldier was at his post by this time and ready for anything, but, about a hundred or more of the native detachment deserted.

Along with their officer! This meant that our numbers were sorely depleted so our positions had to be revised.

We managed to get another two walls erected from biscuit boxes before the enemy were sighted. Hundreds of Zulus were advancing from the south. I was positioned behind the south wall of mealy sacks. Young Charlie was next to me, then Rick, Gus, Morg and Howard. I didn't look any further down the line. It went on as far as the hospital then there was another group guarding the storehouse.

At first they fired from under cover of the Oskaburg hills and the bush. Rifle from the hills continued when the big push began. On they came, running and dodging through the bush area, waving their white shields in front of their black bodies.

What a bizarre sight. They had an ostrich feather coming out of each headband and their chests were covered with beaded necklaces. My blood boiled when I saw how many were wearing the red coats, which must have been taken off our dead comrades. There was one on a white horse; I suppose he must have been a chief. I levelled my Martini-Henry. He was going to be my first target.

As soon as they were in range we fired, then they were falling by the dozen.

When I hit my target, his fat body flopped over his horse. The weight must have been too much for the poor horse, for they both fell to the ground. Or, someone else's bullet hit the horse at the same time that mine hit the chief... On they came, hour upon hour; we kept firing, round after round. The reverend and the commie kept us supplied with bullets, risking their lives, dragging heavy boxes around to the boys behind the lines.

Those Zulus who were not killed got cover by the cookhouse and ovens, from where they fired, volley after volley. One small mercy was that they were not good shots. We heard pings as bullets hit the biscuit boxes and thuds as they pierced mealy sacks. We saw that the hospital thatch roof had been set on fire, and as it was getting dark the fire lit up the whole area. This was a snake with two heads, terrible for the surgeon and his patients but it enabled us to see the enemy as they continued to come at us. After hours of fighting the attacking Zulus withdrew to the base of the hills where they did some sort of ritual dance. A few of us boys were sent backwards to the hospital, where much fighting was still taking place. There was smoke and fumes all around them and bodies were falling everywhere. When I turned I spotted young Billy in front of the hospital. He was re-loading his rifle. A huge black Zulu was running at him, I fired but my shot reached its target too late. The bloody heathen screamed out his war cry, and gutted poor Billy Hopkins. As Billy fell his innards spilled out, and the dead Zulu fell on top of him. I remember running to him and dragging the Zulu off the boy with difficulty, because my hands were burnt through constant firing, and my shoulder was painful. Then, I was oblivious to everything except this poor boy laying at my feet. I sank to my knees and I must have lost my mind or gone crazy for a minute. I felt myself being pulled of Billy's body; I was covered in his blood. I had been trying franticly to push back Billy's guts into his body! The good colour sergeant pulled me back and then put his arm around my shoulder saying, "Come on now, Lewis, there's no more to be done for this poor boy. Pull yourself together now. We must return to our posts, for I don't think they are finished with us yet." That was the one and only time the colour sergeant, used anything but my number. I had thought that we were all just numbers to the officers. He was right about the enemy; they had not finished with us. On they came again and again, until the ground in front of our defences was littered with dead and injured Zulus. I received an injury to the side of my face just below my eye, when a Zulu threw his assegai at me. He did not live to tell the tale! My rifle jammed, so I used my bayonet and thrust as hard as I could into his belly, as he ran at me.

Finally all became quiet. It was early morning. No one dared to move in case they came again. Thankfully, Rick, Morg , Gus and Howard were still with me. We could not speak. Exhausted, we collapsed to the ground alongside each other. We had been fighting for almost fifteen hours. I must have fallen asleep, and so did the others, because the next thing we heard was the sound of mounted infantry, and then we saw the general's column arriving. What relief! Shouts went out from all over the camp. All of us who could stand and walk left our posts and cheered them in. Those who couldn't move, cheered and waved, from where sat or lay. The soldiers who were coming into the camp looked as if they could not believe their eyes! Hundreds of dead black bodies lay around the camp. The smell of burning thatch, combined with the stench of blood and human excretions was sickening. The Kaffirs who came with the relief column were put to work digging a trench for the bodies of the enemy. Three hundred and fifty Zulus needed to be buried. The rest of the Zulus, who we killed before they reached us, had been carried away by their own men. Most of their bodies were taken down to the drift and dropped into the river. We buried our own comrades near to the places where they were killed.

The reverend very kindly said, that later on, a wall could be built around the graves. Then it would be a proper cemetery. I think he also had in mind that some of the injured may need to be buried before too long. The whole camp was in such a mess, but some men managed to boil water for tea. Tins of bully beef were opened and boxes of biscuits, so we had food and a hot drink for breakfast. And a sergeant found a cask of rum which was most welcome. The general set his men to fortifying the camp. He praised 'this brave little garrison' and those who, he said, had fought so bravely.

April 2nd 1879.

My mates and me are in a sorry state. The first months since the big battle have been hard on us. The weather has been wicked, and we had no protection from it, no fresh clothes, blankets, or shelter. The only food we had was the remains of the tinned bully beef and mealy biscuits. There are more than forty men in the hospital, and another sixty needing treatment, for disease, fever and dysentery. I do not know how many have died. I am glad I wrote home in March, telling that I was alive and well. I don't think I would be able to write a line now, which would not cause anxiety to my dear wife or mother.

After the battle of the twenty-second, the general was said to have put in motion plans to send us home. I hope it will be soon, or there will be more of us that don't make it. The surgeon cleaned up my face and put a dressing over my eye. He said he was not able to do more for me with such meagre facilities, and so many patients. It doesn't hurt, I have no feeling in that area except numbness. Another very strange thing has happened. My hair, which I made the barber shave to the skin in January, has grown again. But it's white!

The injured are to be taken to Durban and then sent home, and it seems I am to join them. When I asked to be excluded, I was sent to the surgeon for examination. I thought it was because of the injury to my face and eye. But he told me there was something wrong with my heart! Howard is also to go. He has been told that he too has a bad heart, but he has also been ill with diarrhoea, and he has trouble breathing. I wrote three letters today for the sick and injured, and one boy gave me this piece of paper after I told him I kept a diary, but it was full. I didn't tell him that I tore out the last page to write home.

June 9th 1879.
A kind nurse gave me several sheets of writing paper and pencils. Emma will be surprised when she sees that the paper is headed 'The Royal Military Hospital Chelsea'. This is where we were brought, in haste, after landing at Gibraltar. The journey from Rorke's Drift was not too bad, though I don't remember much of it. We were given clean clothes and supplies before we left the Drift. These were bought from money donated by the grateful people of Pietersmaritzburg. They also provided food and essentials for us. They said that they were grateful, because we stopped the Zulus, preventing them from conquering the whole of the Natal. The army medics made us as comfortable as possible in hospital wagons. We made a few stops at camps on the way. Travelling with oxen pulling the wagons

over some pretty rough terrain, took so long. We sailed from Durban to Gibraltar, travelling by sea. This time was a good deal easier than the last. We had decent beds, and were taken good care of by the medics.

July 11th 1879.

I have been here for quite some time. I must say that the doctors and medics are very good here, but it was a big shock when the surgeon who examined me said I would need to have the eye operation. A clot of blood had formed on the back of my eye and the area had become infected. The operation would involve removing the eye. So he will set a date, as soon as possible for the operation. I did a reconnoitre of the hospital looking for Howard, I found him and several of our comrades close to each other in one of the small wards. They were all on the mend and glad to see me. Young David Rhys had lost a leg. He was being given some sort of medication for stress or depression, because he had been suicidal. He was talking all right but in a daze, as if he wasn't quite all there. I gathered that was because of the medication he had been given. Howard was almost well, but said he had been told his army days were over, he would be going home once the doctor signed him out. He sympathised with me for the loss of my eye, but we all agreed we were the lucky ones. Charlie and a few others were even better off. They had gone home from Gibraltar, with orders to see their local doctors, concerning the possible after effects of warring and wicked living conditions. I left them with the promise to keep in touch, and Howard assured me he would not leave the hospital without seeing me first.

August 11th 1879.
Since the operation I have experienced very little discomfort, they give me doses of something to ease the pain when it comes. But writing is only possible in short bursts, because I get headaches. The surgeon is coming to see me this afternoon to remove the dressing, and check the result. Then if all is well, a special medic will fit me with an artificial, glass eye.

August 17th 1879.
A remarkable man arrived at my bedside today, he introduced himself as Harold. He is the artificial eye specialist. He came to examine the colour of my good eye and the empty socket which has healed nicely. In contrast to his appearance which was of a plump, short man, with a happy round face. The intensity of his stare, was quite unnerving. He spoke with a low voice, explaining

the procedure of fitting a glass eye and the after care.We talked for a while, he was interested to know about Rorke's Drift, which he had read about in the newspapers. Recalling that dreadful day was something I wanted to avoid, so I just gave him a brief account of the Zulu army. I explained that it was too difficult for me to give more details about the fighting as yet. He said he understood and apologised for being so thoughtless. He had not been able to talk to the other soldiers who had come to the hospital, from Africa. I told him that I had seen Howard, who was a comrade, and very good friend of mine, even though we were in different wards. I didn't know the other comrades in my ward well enough to disturb their peace.

August 25th 1879.

Howard was with me today when Harold came to fit my new glass eye. It feels strange, but Harold has got the colour spot on, it's a perfect match. He brought a mirror so I could see how I look. I am going to have to get used to controlling the movement of my eyelid, it sticks on top of the new eye and looks weird. But Harold has told me that this usually happens when these eyes are first fitted. I was soon able to bring my lid half way, so it looks more natural, at least it's better than having an eye patch! Howard told me that when I get it right nobody will know it's false, but I have my doubts.

August 30th 1879.
People from 'The Injury Assessment Board' came to the hospital today. I have been discharged from the army! They gave me a certificate saying: Private David Lewis. Suffering from a vascular disease of the heart, caused by constant exposure to inclement climate variations; long periods under canvas; the strain of fighting in so many battles, including the effects of having to watch comrades, good men, being mutilated and killed during the Zulu wars. My good friend Howard has been told exactly the same. We are both to be given a military pension of six pence per day. We have papers saying all the above, to take with us, when we go home.

August 31st 1879.
This morning I went around a couple of wards saying goodbye and good luck to comrades less fortunate than me. I was shocked to find Rick, Gus and Morg, in Howard's ward, all suffering from the same heart disease as me and Howard. Gus looked rough, Rick and Morg didn't look much better. We had all lost weight during our time in Africa, but these three were shadows of their former selves.

Rick told us that they had stayed with the battalion and had foot slogged, to the main camp at Ulundi. When they arrived they saw the surgeon who said they should have been sent home from Rorke's Drift. On his recommendation they received their discharge and were sent home to be hospitalised. We exchanged news and talked for over an hour at which point Harold came looking for me. He brought me a list of instructions about my new eye. He had been told that I was going home, by military hospital wagon and he wanted to say goodbye. He shook my hand and wished me good luck. When Harold had left it was time for Howard and me to go. It was so hard to leave Rick, Gus and Morg. However we promised to keep in touch.

CHAPTER 9

James arrived home early in the evening on the second of September. He had not had the time or the means to notify Emma of his time of arrival, so she was taken by surprise. She could hardly believe this was the same man who went away almost two years ago. He was wearing his uniform, the only clothing he possessed. He had lost weight, his hair was white, and his skin was still quite sunburnt. "James! Oh my God James, is it really you?" she exclaimed rushing to him with her arms open wide. He caught her up in his arms and hugging her tight he buried his head in her shoulder. Overcome with emotion, he was unable to utter a word for several minutes.

"James, are you all right, my dear, are you still suffering? Have they sent you home too soon?"

Finding his voice James answered her, "I'm fine now my love, I'm home alive and I swear to God I will never leave you again."

"Mammy," came a young voice from upstairs. "Who's down there, Mammy?"

"It's your Daddy come home, Amy. Come on down and Thomas, you bring little David Lewis." Emma looked hard at her husband. "James I hope you are up to this, the children may not recognise you." Before she had finished the sentence Amy was bumping down the stairs, feet first then on her bottom, taking them one at a time. Thomas followed behind with little David Lewis. They each looked at James with the same disbelief. Thomas was the first to speak. "You look so different, James, you're very brown looking, and what happened to your hair?"

"That's a bit of a long story, Thomas, but for now what about my welcome hugs from my beautiful children?" He held out his arms and Thomas went to him with a beaming smile. Amy just stood still and stared at him. Little David Lewis started to cry and toddled to his mother. Emma gathered the child into her arms. "Don't cry, darling, everything is fine, this is your daddy come home from the wars."

"Please don't worry, Emma." James was disappointed, but understood. "It will take time for them to get used to me again. Carry on as normal and just let me enjoy being home with you and the children."

"Right, my dear, just as you like." Emma sighed with relief. "Thomas, you'll have plenty of time with Dad tomorrow and in days to come. David Lewis is all right now so please take him and Amy upstairs to tidy up the toys. Violet will be home soon from granny's and she will help you, and Dad can have a rest after his long journey."

Left alone, James took Emma in his arms and led her to the sofa where they sat holding each other close while he whispered words of love.

First to call the following day were aunt Alice and Emma's parents, Lewis carrying a few beers and some wine, the ladies with baskets full of good things to eat. Alice and Edith hugged and kissed James with tears in their eyes. Lewis shook his hand and they all welcomed him home. They celebrated, and James spent the day enjoying the event and counting his blessings. It was early evening when Edward, big Dai, little Dai, Bryan and Ben arrived. The men each shook his hand in turn, then Edward grabbed him in a bear hug grinning. "Welcome back, cousin. It's so good to see you."

Lewis gave the men a drink and suggested they walk out to the back yard and leave the women to preparing the food.

"We have some privacy out here, boys." Lewis spoke severely. "That gives us the opportunity to break the bad news to James. There is hell of a thing for you to come home to after all you've been through. But I think it's time you learnt the bad news, better from us than from the law. What about you Ben, will you start us off?"

"Right, Lewis. It's like this. You know James, that Tommy Davies was set upon when you left for Brecon?" Ben raised his eyebrows while looking at James, who nodded in agreement. "Well, the attack occurred early in the morning on the day you left home, and the law are going to be questioning you for an alibi. They know that you had a right go at Tommy, so that makes you a massive suspect." Ben paused, before continuing thoughtfully. "What is needed now, James is a concrete alibi for you, proving you was elsewhere."

Lewis intervened. "Emma does not know what time you left. She was fast asleep. If necessary she will no doubt lie for you, but even so that might not be enough. The law have discovered what time you got to Brecon, and they will know roughly how long it took you to get from Swansea to Brecon."

"Look here, James, I owe you my friend," said big Dai. "So if I can help, I will. None of us could blame you if you did give him a hammering."

"That goes for the rest of us boys as well, James," said Edward. "We all agreed that it could have been any one of us — we all hated that sod with a vengeance."

"Well, this is a blow I can't deny," James replied. "But this time it wasn't me. Though I thank you all for such loyalty and friendship."

"The first thing, James boy, is we all believe you when you say you are innocent, but we must prove it," said Lewis. "If it comes to the push, I will get you the best defence available."

"You need time to think, we know that," said Ben, "But the law could come for you before you are ready for them. The first thing they will ask is where were you at the time of Tommy's attack?"

"Bloody hell, Ben, I left before the crack of dawn. I don't even know what time it was. I remember walking through the deserted streets, and watching lights going on in houses when I got near to Neath." James' voice echoed his concern. "I walked all the way on my own. I do remember going to sleep on the beacons and making my way down the following morning. One thing I'm sure of Lewis, is my Emma must not be asked to lie. In the first place she is no good at lying and I cannot stomach the thought of making her."

"Come on, you lot, the food is ready," called Edith from the house.

"Right boys no more talk for now," Lewis ordered. "At least James will be more prepared now if he gets questioned. But I do urge you to talk to

Emma, and prepare her for a visit by the law, James."

When the guests had all left, James told Emma what he and the men had discussed.

"Oh my God, James, murder! How will you prove you didn't do it?"

"The thing is, my love, they can't prove I did because I'm innocent," James said trying to convince himself as well as her. "So you are not to worry, come to bed now and we'll face things as they come."

Three days went by, during which James and Emma received a constant stream of friends and well-wishers. This gave them very little time, in the day to worry about the law. It was during the nights that they lay awake wondering if or rather when the police would come for him.

They knocked on his door on the fourth day, two of them, a young constable and a sergeant. James answered the door knock and let them in. They were both well-built men of medium height. The young Constable was clean shaven with dark hair and brown eyes. He stood a little behind his boss and remained silent. The Sergeant had slightly lighter hair, hazel eyes and sported a military style moustache. "I am Sergeant Michael Wallis and this is Constable Sidney Brown. You, I gather, are James Owen." When James simply nodded the sergeant continued, "We are here to take you to the station for questioning concerning the murder of a Mr Tommy Davies. I warn you that anything you say will be noted and may be used against you as evidence."

James turned to his wife. "Now, lovely girl, you must try not to worry. I have go with the policemen. You need to go to your father and tell him what has happened. Take care of yourself and the children until I come back." He hugged and kissed her. "You'll be all right, my Emma, please tell me you'll be all right."

Emma couldn't speak, she felt as if she were choking, holding back the tears that threatened. She hugged him tightly and kissed his face, his neck and then his face again. James kissed her back and then gently pushed her away saying, "I really need you to be brave for us now, my love."

The police station was a large converted house in the centre of town. James was taken past a desk where two policemen were talking to a group of young boys. They walked him through a passage, which led into a small room with a table and two chairs, one either side of the table.

"You will take a seat this side of the table, Mr Owen and you, constable, will wait here with Mr Owen until I return," said the sergeant.

James sat and waited, nervously crossing and uncrossing his legs. He looked at the young constable who seemed familiar to him. "Do I know you from somewhere, constable? Only I think I recognise your face."

"Yes, Mr Owen, I'm Sid Brown — we met briefly years ago on a trip to the beach." The young man's voice held an apologetic tone. "I was the boy with Bobby, when you saved him from drowning. You were a hero that day and you're a hero now come back from a war." He paused thoughtfully. "I'm not supposed to be talking to you, though I must say that I am very sorry to see you in this trouble. And I wish it had been somebody else chosen to go with the sergeant today."

"Don't you worry, Sid boy, I understand you have a job to do." James tried to sound sympathetic. However, he was at present much too concerned with his own worries. He wished the sergeant would come back — this waiting was making him most anxious.

Eventually the sergeant returned looking very red faced. "Mr Lewis Davies has come to the station with a lawyer to see you," he said sounding annoyed. "I told Mr Davies that this is not a hospital with visiting. He will not be allowed to see you. And it is your choice whether or not you see this lawyer chap. So what do you say, shall I bring him in?"

"Why, yes if you please, sergeant, I very much need to talk to someone," James answered. A few minutes went by before the sergeant returned with a very smartly dressed, middle-aged man. He looked every inch a professional, with his short fair hair neatly groomed, and his penetrating blue eyes looking through spectacles.

"Stay where you are, constable," the sergeant ordered young Sid. "I will be back in half an hour. This will be enough time for you?" he asked the lawyer.

"And if it's not?" returned the lawyer, raising his eyebrows.

The sergeant, ignoring this last question went out and closed the door. Not quite with a bang, but heavy enough to make the door shudder. The lawyer held out his hand and introduced himself to James. "My name is Arnold Dawson, and your good father-in-law has hired me to defend you. I suggest we get straight down to the business in hand. I need you to give me accurate details, of your movements, on the morning of the seventh of the twelfth eighteen seventy six, between the hours of six a.m. and seven thirty.

"Right, sir, the thing is I cannot be completely accurate about the time, Mr Dawson," James answered, trying his best to remember. He continued, "I know the streets were deserted when I left the house, and it was still dark. So it was probably well before five. Then as I walked through Neath I remember that lights went on in a few of the houses. The streets were still empty and it was quiet, so I still couldn't tell what time it was, but when I think again dawn was breaking. Also I know is that it was night time again when I reached the top of the Beacons when I slept. Not much help am I, Mr. Dawson?"

"Did you see anyone you would recognise again, or who would possibly recognise you, during your walk?" asked his lawyer. "By the way, James, we are going to get to know each other quite well so I suggest you start calling me Arnold."

"Right, I will, thank you Arnold. As for the walk, there were people around by the time I got to Neath but I didn't know any of them. The only person I spoke to was when I stopped to rest, and sat on a bench just inside a cemetery.

"A gentleman sat with me and shared his hot tea while we ate our packed food." James paused trying to remember the man's name. "I've got it, he told me his name was Albert Morris and we talked for a while. Now I wish I had asked him the time because I remember he had a posh pocket watch."

"Very good, James, now we could be getting somewhere," the lawyer replied, writing, in a note book with pencil. "Think again, was there anyone or anything else, during your walk that you can think of."

"There was no one I'm sure. Not that I can remember anyway." James' voice was beginning to sound despondent.

"Take your time now, my lad, we have but started. There is much to be carefully thought through, so you must be patient. So, what can you remember, if anything about the man you met at the cemetery?" Arnold asked patiently.

"He spoke about his wife and sons who were buried there. They died as a result of the cholera outbreak." Still feeling inadequate James racked his brain for useful information. "Come to think of it, he did say that he visits the cemetery the same time every day. That means he would know what the time was when we sat together. But is that any help to us?"

"This last item of information might well be critical James. We can calculate how long it would take to walk from Swansea to this cemetery you speak of." Arnold stopped and he wrote again in his note book. "Would you know the name of the cemetery or the road it was on?"

"No, but if I could go that way again I would know it," James said anxiously.

"That may not be possible, James," Arnold became very serious. "I am sure you will have to spend a time incarcerated, because, as yet, you are the number one suspect."

"You do mean I am to go to jail, Arnold?" said a very downhearted James.

"That seems likely, my man. First you will be put into a cell here in this station until a date is given for you to appear in court. The case will no doubt go to trial. Before this, Lewis and I will try for bail. Lewis is prepared to act as bail bondsman, which as you probably know is that the judge will set an amount and Lewis will agree to pay. From now on, James, you must keep trying to remember facts which could help in your defence. I will prepare your defence and see you every day possible. We have covered all we can for now and the sergeant has given us some overtime, so I will say goodbye for now."

James shook Arnold's hand vigorously "Thank you very much and thank you for believing I'm innocent."

"Do not assume I believe you are innocent, James. I met you for the first time today. I must work to prove your innocence to myself as well as to the judge."

Constable Brown opened the door for the lawyer, who said thank you as he left. The sergeant returned saying to Sidney, "You and me are going to take the prisoner to the cells now, constable."

"And I hope you will come quietly, Mr Owen."

There were only three small 'holding cells', these were for prisoners awaiting court appearance. Each cell had four bunks and a bucket for obvious use. James was taken to the middle cell, where two men were sitting one on each of the bottom bunks. When the sergeant locked the cell door James felt his first taste of panic. Until now the events following his arrest were surreal. He had simply gone through the necessary motions. James moved towards the upper bunks when the elder of the two men spoke to him. "Sit down here for a minute boy," he said, indicating a small space at his side. His great bulk covered a large area of the bed. "I'm Dan and he's Freddy. Tell us, first who you are, and what you're in for."

"My name is James Owen and I've been arrested for a murder which I did not commit," James answered looking first at one and then the other. They were both evidently in need of a bath, or at least a good wash — the smell of body odour filled the cell. The younger man looked to be about nineteen but it was hard to tell because his face was almost covered with cuts and bruises. *'I wouldn't like to meet either of you in a dark alley,'* thought James.

The man who called himself Dan grinned showing yellow teeth with several gaps. "Oh yes? Innocent are you, just like all the rest of us in here. We'll believe you though won't we, Freddy?"

Freddy winced as he tried to smile, "Don't make me laugh, Dan, you know it hurts my face in this state."

The following day Lewis paid a visit to a judge of his close acquaintance who lived in the posh Sketty area of Swansea, near to Lewiss' house. The housekeeper answered Lewis's knock. "Hello Mabel," he said smiling at the homely woman. "You are looking good. Over your bad cold I see."

"Hello Mr Davies, nice to see you. I'm fine now thanks." She returned his smile. "Come on through, he's in his room he calls the home office."

The honourable Judge Paul Ford was sitting at his desk, which was very neat, with the exception of the file he was working on.

"Good morning, Lewis," said the judge rising to shake his friend's hand. "To what do I owe this unexpected pleasure?"

"Good morning to you, Paul. I have a problem that I desperately hope you can help me with." Lewis spoke slowly and thoughtfully. "My son-in-law has been arrested for a murder he did not commit. He is at present being held over in the police station and I need to get him out on bail. What must I do? And is there any way you can help?"

"Murder charge you say, Lewis? Has he been given a date for the court hearing?" Judge Paul asked. "And have you sought legal advice?"

"Of course the court hearing must come first. I had forgotten that, Paul." Lewis had known this, but he was so desperate for help that he had chosen to 'jump the gun'. "I have hired Arnold Dawson. I believe he is known to you"

"Yes, I know the man, and in my opinion you have done well to secure his services. As to the hearing, I have not been approached, so it depends on which of my colleagues is on the bench." Stopping for a moment, Judge Paul continued thoughtfully, "My good friend John Banks is as straight as they come, if he thinks your boy is dangerous he will not allow bail. However, he is also a reasonable man who has allowed bail on many occasions. However, should Judge Ryan Phillips, be on the bench, the situation changes. He has very rarely allowed bail and never when there is a charge of murder in court."

"I see, Paul, will it help if Arnold knows which judge will preside?" Lewis asked, hoping to be told which judge it would be.

"It may well do, Lewis. Once we have the date of the hearing, I will ask my friend John if he is going to preside. That is as far as I can go to help you."

"Thank you, Paul, I can assure you that James is not only a decent man, he is also a war hero just returned from Africa. Do you remember the stories about him in the local newspapers, when he fought in the famous Battle of Rorke's Drift ."

"Yes, I do and I also remember saying how proud you Edith and Emma must be. That will gain him a certain amount of goodwill, but I doubt it will have much effect on his defence," Judge Paul said sympathetically. "Will you try to relax for just a moment and take a drink with me, Lewis?" Not waiting for an answer Judge Paul stood and walked over to a the table laden with several bottles and glasses. "Come now, whisky neat, or with a splash of water?"

Lewis stayed with his friend long enough to enjoy a glass of good malt whisky then he left in a less hopeful frame of mind. He was now anxious about who was to be the presiding judge at James' hearing.

Edith was disappointed to learn what had occurred during Lewis' visit to the judge. She had hoped that their friend would be James' judge.

As promised James' lawyer, Arnold, arrived each day to speak with James. It was not until the third day that he told James of an interesting development. "I was approached yesterday by a group of your friends, James. They were anxious to know how they could help you. I explained that what we needed was to find the old man who could possibly provide you with an alibi. The one called big Dai was the first to offer his services. He promised to find the cemetery in question and speak to the old man you met. The other three or maybe four men agreed to help." Arnold rubbed his chin deep in thought. "I think there were four of them. You have good friends in there, James, but they are working men and will need to scout during the evenings or leisure time. I did tell them that your hearing has been set for three days' time, so the sooner our witness is found the better for you."

"They are good friends, Arnold, I would put my trust in any one of them. So if Albert is still alive and can be found they will find him," James assured him.

"I am sure your right, James, I was impressed by their loyalty to you," Arnold said nodding. " In the meantime we must prepare a submission for the court with regard to our application for bail. We will need character witnesses. Your cousin Edward advised me to contact a Mr Dewy Lloyd. I am aware that he dismissed you as a result of your action against the victim. However, he will testify that you were severely provoked, and that prior to this event you were an exemplary employee." Taking out his notepad and pencil the lawyer said, "We need at least one, maybe more witnesses to speak on your behalf, James. Who do you suggest? Bear in mind, it must be someone respectable and of good standing in the community."

"There is my old friend and tutor, Reverend Thomas. He has known me since I was a boy, and he is an honourable man." James answered. "And what about Lewis, can we call on him?"

"I'm afraid not James. Lewis being a relative cannot be considered." Arnold shook his head, frowning. "But the minister you speak of, fits the criteria required and I will ask Lewis to inform the good man. I hope he will be able to make the hearing. I must leave you now, James, I have a busy day ahead. Please continue to rack your brain for another witness which we may well need."

Big Dai decided he would take time off from work and go to Neath the following morning. Edward, Ben, little Dai, Bryan, and young Henry, all agreed that if Edward spoke to the boss, they would each take on extra work, without pay, while big Dai is away. They also agreed to club together for the train money to take big Dai to Neath and back.

The first train in the morning left at eight o' clock with big Dai aboard. When he arrived at Neath Station there were crowds of working people waiting for the train which was going on to Cardiff. He waited for the crowd to thin out before he spoke to the station master. "Good morning to you, sir," said Dai politely. "I wonder if you can help me. I need to visit a cemetery in Neath. I am afraid I don't know the name of the cemetery or even the road it's on. I am a stranger to the place you see."

The station master looked kindly at the young man in front of him, answering with a frown. "That happens to be a tall order son, there are three cemeteries around here, but they are not close together. The nearest one is just a short walk up the main street, the next one is about half an hour walk, and the third about the same from there. I've lived here all my life, so I should know. Come to the little office and I'll write down some directions for you." Dai couldn't believe his luck as he followed the kind man to the office. When he was given excellent directions he suddenly had a thought. "If I was walking from Swansea, sir, do you know which one I would come to first?"

"Well now, let me think. I suppose that would be on the Neath South Road, this one," he said pointing to the second cemetery on his list."

"Thank you very much, sir. You have been so kind. With your helpful directions I am sure I will find my way." said Dai before going on his way.

Arriving at the cemetery, Dai found what he thought, could be the bench seat that James had described. There was no one about so he decided to and wait a while. He ate his sandwiches and was drinking his water when he heard footsteps. A strange looking woman came into the cemetery. He couldn't stop staring at her. She was wearing a long billowing black skirt and a pair of manly boots. Her head and face were covered by a floppy hat, and the top half of her body was wrapped in a shawl with more holes in it than his father's socks. Thinking she may be a regular visitor here, and able to help he spoke to her. "Good day to you, missus."

She lifted the front of her hat folding it back to reveal a thin wrinkled face. "Good day back to you then," she answered with a squeaky voice.

"I wonder if you can help me please. I am looking for an old man who used to come and sit here every day." She was staring at him in such a strange way that Dai began to wonder if she was 'loose in the attic'.

"What do you want with old Albert then, not in trouble is he? No he can't be, because he was a policeman. So what then?" Her strange way of talking matched her appearance.

"No trouble I promise you," Dai answered. "I just want to talk to him about something he might help me with."

"You won't find him ever at this time, he's always gone by now. When he does come, it's always at half past seven. That's where his family is buried," she said pointing to a nearby grave.

"Right, but do you know where I might find him?" Dai was beginning to feel desperate.

"Not me," she squeaked even higher. "You won't find me talking about Albert Morris." She began to cackle like an old hen as she walked on. Dai was at a loss for ideas on what he could do now, when he wondered if there would be anyone on the street who would know this elusive Albert.

He walked around road after road, for hours asking people for help. Several of them knew Albert Morris and the fact that he had recently moved house. But, not one of them knew where he had moved to. By early evening he was almost at the end of his tether, but Dai was not going to give up. He decided to go home tonight and come back again tomorrow. The same station master had just finished his shift and was on his way out as Dai arrived at the station. "Hello again, young man," he said. "How did you get on today?"

"I found the cemetery easily thanks to you, sir. No luck with the man I was looking for though. So you will be seeing me again tomorrow. By the way, sir, is there an earlier train than the eight o'clock from Swansea?"

"There are two goods trams that stop down the loading bay, coming at six and six-thirty a.m. They sometimes bring livestock as well so they can be smelly and uncomfortable."

"That won't bother me as long as I can start out earlier than today." Dai told a small untruth, because he had an aversion to live geese, chickens, and ducks.

When Dai arrived back home he found Edward and little Dai talking to his wife Elsie and his son Billy.

"Was it all right today big man? Little Dai came with me to find out how you got on."

"All right, Edward, you all right, little Dai?" returned big Dai as he spoke he moved towards his wife and kissed her on the cheek. "You all right, Elsie girl?"

"I'm just fine now you're home my man. I'd better put your dinner in the oven to warm, while you talk to the men."

"Right my friends. First of all the station master in Neath gave me good directions, so I found the cemetery and the bench seat that James told us about. Then I met a crazy old woman who cackled like a hen. She told me that the old man Albert is always at the cemetery, at seven thirty. I tried to find somebody who knew him by walking the streets, and I talked to a few, who told me he had moved house. But no one knew where he lived now and that's it in a nutshell. I will try again tomorrow, but I'll have to catch the early goods tram."

Edward, who had listened carefully as Dai spoke, asked, "What about this station master bloke, my friend, did you think that maybe he would know the old man?"

Dai gasped and his eyebrows rose. "What a bloody fool I am not to think of that. Sorry for the swearing, love." He grinned sheepishly when Elsie frowned at him.

"Not to worry, Dai, you can talk to him tomorrow. I went down to Llanboidy today with Lewis. We saw the vicar and he promised to be at the hearing to speak for James. Then we went to see James' family," said Edward. "Lewis told David and Anne about the bail — he was trying to make the situation a bit easier for them. Anne is worried sick, but then women show more than men. I think David is only just holding up."

"I hope you don't mind me barging in, boys, but my man's dinner is going to spoil," said Elsie with a tray of food in her hands.

"We were finished anyway, Elsie. Enjoy your dinner then Dai, and we'll see you tomorrow. That will be it then because the hearing is the day after. Have a good night now, good night to you too, Elsie, and Billy."

The following day while Dai continued his search, Arnold Dawson entered the police question room where James was waiting impatiently. "We seem to be getting somewhere, James. The minister you spoke of has agreed to testify. However, your good friend has had no luck in finding our witness. He did find the cemetery and bench seat, but as yet no sign of the old man. He will try again today, but I fear we will need to proceed without the hope of finding him in time."

"Does this mean that you have lost confidence in our chance of bail, Arnold?" asked a very anxious James.

"Not at all young man, there is your minister, who will I'm sure impress the judge. Also I am prepared to address the judge concerning your bravery during the African wars. I have been informed that Judge John Banks will preside over the hearing. This particular judge has approved several of my bail requests in the past. However, I cannot find evidence of bail being given by him to a prisoner charged with murder. But I could be wrong, and I am sure he will appreciate that you are man of good character and social status, so don't despair."

When Arnold left James was returned to his cell and his freakish companions. "Your posh lawyer going to get you out tomorrow then boy, is he?" Dan growled. He was sitting on the edge of his bed, leaning forward like an animal ready to pounce.

James was not afraid. He stood still, thrust out his chest and tensed his body, thinking that this was the climax which they had been building up to since his arrival. He knew he could take care of himself against this ugly bastard. He just hoped that Freddy would not join his mate.

"Take it easy, for God's sake, Dan," Freddy intervened, hoping to calm the man down. "Hold your bloody horses, we're in enough crap without you making it worse." Dan turned and growled at Freddy, before he sat back on his bed. James climbed on to his bunk bed and stayed awake until he heard the other two snoring.

Arnold arrived early at the police station in the morning of James' court hearing. The sergeant was nowhere to be found so he approached Constable Brown. "Good day to you, constable. I have brought a clean shirt, shaving soap and razor for James Owen. I need him to look respectable for his hearing today. Would you be able to fill this mug with hot water please, constable?"

"The hot water will not be a problem, sir, but I cannot not permit you to take a razor into the cell. You should know better than to ask, you being a lawman."

"Why certainly I would not wish to do such a thing, particularly as I have met James' cell mates! No indeed, I was hoping we could take James into the questioning room."

"I would be breaking all the rules and risking my job. But I suppose I could talk to my sergeant. The thing is, between you and me, I would like to do something for Mr Owen." The young man's discomfort echoed in his voice.

"I did look for your sergeant, but he is nowhere to be found. And I would appreciate your help for the good of my client." Arnold pressed his request in the hope of the constable acting in his favour, before the return of the sergeant.

The young man thought for a minute or two before saying, "I could take you to the prisoners' washroom and lock you in for a short while, and pretend that I do not know about the razor. What about that?"

"Excellent idea, Sid, is it all right for me to call you Sid?"

"I suppose so, when there's no one about though, if you don't mind."

"Good thinking, my man. Shall we go then?" prompted the lawyer.

When they arrived at James' cell Arnold was told to wait, out of sight, until the constable brought James out. "I want you to come with me, Mr Owen," said the constable, as he unlocked the cell door. James readily obliged wondering what was going on, but saying nothing. "I guessed that you would want to clean up this morning," said Sid, in a loud enough to be overheard. "So I am taking you to the washroom."

"What about us, then?" was a shout from Dan.

"When your lawyer gets permission," was Sid's loud answer.

James was surprised when he saw Arnold waiting for them. "What's happening now?" he whispered as they walked. Arnold shook his head, and frowned, directing James to keep silent. Sid opened the washroom door saying, "You have to be pretty quick. I'll lock the door and stay here 'til you knock."

Less than ten minutes later James emerged a new man. Arnold smiled at the relieved look on Sid's face. "I will take you to the question room now, where you can stay 'til it's time for the court."

"Thank so very much, Sid. Arnold has told me what a risk you took. I am deeply in your debt, my friend," James said, moved by the young man's effort to help him.

Once they were seated in the question room Arnold took out his briefcase saying, "Your good friend spent another fruitless day searching for our witness, which we will go into at another time. For today we will concentrate on your acceptability for bail." Arnold continued to inform James of his prepared submission, while a silent James simply gave the occasional nod in agreement.

They had more or less finished when the sergeant arrived, looking somewhat flustered.

"The constable told me that he gave you time in the washroom. Reasonable prisoners are given this consideration once a week. But you must have noticed that your cell mates have not had, or even wanted, this privilege."

"We quite understand, sergeant," said Arnold, thinking that more of an effort should have been made for the sake of hygiene. "However I think the time has come for me to leave you. I will see you in court then James. Will you be bringing James in, sergeant, or will that be the duty of another officer?"

"I will accompany the prisoner. His cell mates are also up for hearing, so there will be four constables with us." answered the sergeant.

The courtroom reflected the age of the building with low ceilings exposing wide beams. But the walls were decorated with green and white wallpaper, which was new, in contrast with the tired furniture. At one end of room there was a broad leather armchair, behind a sizeable oak desk — both looked to have been well used. A few feet away there was a table and chair facing the desk. Behind and to the right of this was another longer table, in front of three chairs. A large bureau stood against one wall, and several chairs had been placed against the opposite wall. The new double doors created the main entrance: there was also a door which led to the judge's chambers, and there was a back door behind the judge's desk. This was where the prisoners entered. James, Dan and Freddy, were taken to a small room next to the courtroom. Dan was first to be called into court, followed shortly after by Freddy. James was left with just the sergeant for company. However, he was too nervous to speak, and his companion showed no desire for conversation, so they both sat in silence. Eventually James Owen was called for.

He was taken to table where his lawyer and a stranger sat waiting for him. Arnold was busy laying papers out on the table when he heard the back door open. He looked up and he was not surprised to see that James looked pale and anxious. He nodded and moved the chair next to him for James to sit down.

They were alone in the room for a few minutes, which was enough for Arnold to settle James down. Suddenly the front doors opened and in came the officers of the court. A well-dressed lady was accompanied by a stern looking man dressed in a black suit with a white shirt. They made their way to the small table, the man carrying one of the spare chairs with him.

Three constables and two robust men in plain clothes, sat either side of the main doors. Arnold turned to James saying, "They have no doubt had a nice tea break while we were kept waiting. That bodes well for us because the judge will also have had a good break. Add that to the fact, that after dealing with the last two you will be seen in a better light."

When the judge entered everyone rose. James took a good look at the man who was going to preside. Judge John Banks wore a wig and a copious black gown. His brown eyes, which were set in a round face, gave nothing away. His mouth was serious and over his top lip he sported a thin brown moustache flecked with grey hairs. He sat down and put on a pair of small round spectacles, then he began to read the documents set before him. A short silence followed while he was reading.

"I have considered all the evidence put before me with regard to the case of the crown versus James Owen. And my decision, considering the lack of alibi, is that the case must go to trial." The judge lowered his spectacles and looked towards Arnold. "That is unless the defence has further evidence for my consideration. Well, counsellor?"

"Not at this time, your honour. We are in the process of tracking down a witness, who will prove my client's innocence. In the meantime I hope you will consider our petition for bail. I have submitted written affidavits, confirming the excellent character of the defendant, from men who are pillars of society. They are both in the outside corridor should you wish to interview them."

"That will not be necessary, counsellor. I have read both documents and I am satisfied that the accused is not a danger to society. Therefore I will allow the accused to be released on bail under the supervision of Mr Lewis Davies. Bail is set at the sum of twenty guineas. The accused will appear before the county court judge during the next sessions," and bang went the judge's gavel. Arnold grinned at James. "So far, so good," he said. " Now we have to find the elusive witness, who is crucial to your defence."

"I am thankful that I don't have to go back and face that pair of freaks again. I swear there would have been another massive fight," said a relieved James. "Do you know what happened to them, Arnold?"

"No, James, I don't," replied the lawyer. " It's my guess that they are both habitual prisoners. I suggest we forget them and make haste to finalise your bail. Your father-in-law is outside waiting with his pony and trap. I will go and bring him in. Once Lewis has settled the bail requirements, you will be able to join your family until the trial."

Lewis was standing beside the horse when Arnold left the court. "Bail has been granted, to the tune of twenty guineas, and he is bound over to your care until the trial," said Arnold. Once the formalities were complete Lewis and James thanked the lawyer and agreed to meet him again in three days' time. This was to give James a few days' respite, and Arnold time to begin working on James' defence.

Emma was waiting at home for news of James' hearing. Her mother and Aunt Alice were there to support her — they also helped to keep the children occupied.

Edith was first to recognise the sound of her husband driving up in the pony and trap. "That will be Lewis now, my dear," she said. "Will you be all right whatever happens Emma? Should I take the children out?" she added, thinking the news might not be good.

"No need, thanks, Mother, I'm...Emma stopped suddenly as her husband walked through the door. "James," she cried, throwing herself into his arms. "Thank God, your back, safe and sound."

"Yes, my love, and it's sorry I am to have worried you again." His apology came from the heart.

"Don't you mind me, I was just distressed about you in that dreadful place," she said. "And I was afraid that you might have to go back."

"Edith, my dear," said Lewis. "Once James has had a little time with the children, shall we take them home with us for tonight? I'm thinking that James and Emma could do with some time alone."

"What a good idea," replied his wife. "Would you all like that?"

"That would have been nice, granny Edith," said Violet. "But me and Thomas are going to granny MacIndow's tonight, if you don't mind."

"I don't mind at all, Violet," Edith replied. "Shall we take the little ones, Emma?"

"That would be good of you both," Emma replied. Alice, who had been a silent observer until now said, "Why don't you pour James a glass of the brandy I brought you Emma, and have one yourself. I'll help Violet with an overnight bag for her and Thomas. Edith can sort out the necessary for little Amy and David Lewis."

"Thanks, Alice. Will you join us in a drink, Dad, while you wait for mother?" Emma asked as she made her way to the kitchen.

"No thanks, love, I just want to have a last word with James. You can go and pour the drinks, for James and yourself."

When everyone was out of earshot Lewis spoke to James. "Are you going to tell Emma tonight about the coming trial James?"

"Doesn't she know about the bail and the arrangements you have made for me then?" James replied.

"Yes, she does, but she doesn't know that the trial will be so soon. The next sessions are in three weeks' time." Lewis answered.

"Right Lewis, I will explain it all to her when you're all gone."

"At last," James gasped. "I love them all, but I can't say I'm sorry they've gone. Now that we are alone, Emma love, there are things we must talk about"

James gave Emma a detailed account of the hearing and informed her of the forthcoming trial. Finally he assured her that they would find the witness and he was confident the nice old man would testify for him.

Emma began to look worried. "I haven't had a chance to tell you 'til now, James, that big Dai came late this afternoon. He said to tell you that he hasn't found the old man yet but he has got his address, and he found the house. Not that it did much good because he got no answer to his knocking of the door."

"I will find him myself, love, so don't worry. I'll get the address from Dai, and if necessary, I will go to the cemetery as often as it takes. Because I know he will turn up to look after his family grave," James reassured her. "Now my love let's enjoy our drink and go to bed. I can't wait to take you in my arms and tell you how much I've missed you."

CHAPTER 10

Big Dai accompanied his friend the following day. Although James found the goods train a distraction from his troubles, it was not an enjoyable one. Several farmers had chosen this day to transport livestock. The noise from gaggling geese and clucking hens made conversation impossible. Arriving shortly after seven a.m. they saw the station master, who was at the other end of the station. Dai suggested they resist approaching him, because they were both eager to get to the cemetery. They reached their destination in good time, and sat down hoping they would not have too long to wait.

James was beginning to lose heart, when the weird old woman arrived. She saw them, and she looked hard at them. "If you are still looking for old Albert Morris you won't find him here," she squeaked.

James felt uncomfortable as, besides looking quite mad, she smelled of stale urine. Nevertheless, faking interest in her he smiled, and said, "I wonder, Ma'am, if you could tell us where we will find him?"

"He's in the infirmary, has been this past week. Broken his leg he has, and had a funny turn. And that's all I am telling you." She walked away cackling as she did before.

"Ma'am," James called after her. "Could you please direct us to the infirmary?"

"No." she shrieked, without looking back. "Find it your bloody selves."

"Looks as if we're off again, James, this old Albert is hard to find. But find him we must, so let's go," Dai said.

"Right then," said James, rising to his feet "We're sure to come across somebody who'll know the way to the infirmary." As luck would have it, the first people they saw, outside the entrance to the cemetery, were a couple with two children. James approached the gentleman. "Excuse me, sir, we are looking for the infirmary. I wonder if you could help us?"

"You're almost on top of it, boys," said the gentleman. "Go down this road and it's the first turning on your right. It's the big grey building, you can't miss it."

James thanked the gentleman for his help and said to Dai, "At last, we're getting a break my friend. I had visions of us having to traipse all over

Neath. Meeting that man was a bit of good luck ."
Their good luck ended there, though. When they
inquired at the infirmary for Mr Albert Morris, they
were told that he could not have visitors for at least
a week. The operation on his leg had been
successful, but he had also received a severe blow
to his head and the surgeon was keeping him under
observation.

"There's nothing else for it, James," said Dai.
"We'll have to call it a day, for today."

"I know, Dai. Let's go home then," replied his
dejected friend.

Arnold Dawson assured James, when they met
the following day, that all was not lost. To the
contrary, Albert could be restored to good health in
time for the trial. Failing that he may just recover
enough to sign an affidavit.

"He is quite an old man, Arnold, I am not so
sure his recovery is going to be soon enough,"
James replied. "I won't give up hope, even though
I seem to be grasping at one particular straw. Tell
me honestly now, how do I stand without Albert?"

"The way I see it, James, is this. With Albert
we have an excellent case, without him we will
need to put our thinking caps on. It comes to mind
that there may be someone else who saw you that
morning. Someone that you were not aware of
perhaps. Try to think of anyone who may have been

about. Question your family and friends, perhaps they can help, and in the meantime I will make my own enquiries."

Albert Morris felt the pain in his leg was getting easier to endure. His favourite nurse had helped him to wash and shave this morning. "Thank you my dear, I feel so much better now," he said, looking up to the tall, slim young woman.

Nurse Lilly Brent straightened her starched apron, and pushed back a lock of fair hair which had escaped from her cap. "There were two young men asking after you last week Albert. I heard them talking to Bryan by the front desk, they had Swansea accents. Do you know who they could be?"

"I can't think of anyone, Lilly. What did they look like?" he responded.

"They were both good looking young men, both quite well built. One very tall and the other, he must be about six foot, and handsome. He had a young face but his hair was as white as yours, and he spoke so nice, not posh, but educated like. Come to think of it though, I didn't hear the very tall one speak at all."

"Typical woman you are, Lilly, all eyes for a handsome bloke," said Albert grinning. "I can't think of any young men like that who would care about me."

Nurse Lilly blushed, thinking Albert was right in saying she concentrated on the handsome man. In fact all she remembered about the other one was that he was incredibly tall.

"Are you all right now then, Albert?" Lilly asked.

"I'm all right, Lilly, but there is something bothering me," he said frowning. "It's my wife and boys you see. Their grave will be neglected since I've been in here. Is there any way you could get me there with a few flowers? I was thinking that if we could borrow one of those chairs, the ones with wheels. Maybe you would be kind enough to take me, when you have time that is."

"Oh my word, Albert, what a request," she replied. "I would love to help you out. The thing is I would need permission to borrow a wheelchair, which should be all right, but I don't know if your doctor will allow such an outing for you. But stop your fretting now, though I'm not promising anything, I'll see what I can do." Two days later Nurse Lilly arrived at Albert's bedside with a wheelchair and a posy of flowers.

Albert beamed at her, "You did it girl. I bet the doctor and the wheelchair man couldn't resist your lovely smile and those gorgeous blue eyes."

"That's enough of that nonsense, Albert. We must be serious now. I promised the doctor that you would be sensible and not get over excited. And that we would go straight to the cemetery and back within half an hour. It's lucky that the cemetery is so close."

Albert, with Lilly's help, rode to the cemetery, enjoying the fresh air and smiling to people passing by. When they arrived Albert gasped in surprise. His wife and sons grave was pristine, with colourful wild flowers arranged in a circle on the surface. "I can't believe my eyes," said Albert. "What kind soul could have done this?"

"Well, this is a nice surprise for you, Albert," said Lilly. "Someone must have known you were ill, and unable to come here."

"But who would that be?" Albert said. "My close friends are all gone, and the only family I have now are cousins who I never see. This is strange, still I'm so pleased, now we can add the flowers that we brought and my darling's grave will look wonderful." His pleasure was dampened as he began to feel unwell so he said to Lilly, "I'm ready to go back now, dear. Thank you again for bringing me."

Eight days had passed since James had made enquiries at the Neath Infirmary. And no progress had been made by any of the numerous people involved in their efforts to find another witness for his defence. Deciding it was time to take matters into his own hands James caught the early goods train to Neath, this time alone. He told Emma his plan on the night before he left, stressing that he wanted to keep this trip between the two of them.

The same attendant was at the reception desk when he arrived. In answer to James' enquiry the attendant hesitated before asking James if he was related to Albert.

"No, sir, I am not a relative, although I am an acquaintance, deeply concerned about Albert's progress," James answered sincerely.

"In that case I will have a word with Albert's nurse. She is a very good nurse and a nice young woman. I'm sure she will speak to you. Wait here while I go and get her." He then left James.

The attendant soon returned accompanied by a tall young nurse. She approached James with a smile. "I am Albert's nurse, Lilly Brent," she said. "We have a small family waiting room which we use to discuss patients progress. I think that we should make our way there, if you want news of Albert." James followed her, to the waiting room across the passage, still feeling perplexed. "Please sit down Mr…?"

"Sorry, I should have introduced myself before. My name is James Owen. I am recently home from the army, I live with my wife and children in Swansea," James told her. The last time I came to see Albert I was told the leg operation was a success, but he had a head injury which needed further observation."

"That's right, Mr Owen. Unfortunately, Albert had a setback in the form of a slight stroke, a few days ago. The doctor prescribed rest and medication for at least another two weeks. Because he lives alone, we are hoping to keep him here longer. That is unless his bed is needed for an emergency. I don't think there is any more I can tell you." James thought she sounded kind so he decided to ask, "Is there any chance of my being able to see him?"

"I'm sorry, Mr Owen," she said. "Not only would it be more than my job is worth, but I care about Albert and I won't risk causing him a setback."

James was devastated. He stopped to think, then in desperation he asked, "Could he be asked to sign a legal document for me?" Seeing the look of amazement on her face he continued with, "I'd better explain, so that you will understand my strange request."

James told the young woman of his walk to Brecon. Stopping at the cemetery and his meeting with Albert.

"I have been accused of a murder I did not commit and Albert is the only person who can provide me with an alibi. If he is able to testify that I was with him at the time."

"Oh my God. This is much more serious than I expected." She looked horrified. "All I can think of is that if you give me the paper, I'll see if I can get him to sign it."

Arnold was waiting in his office for James when in walked Edward. "Good Morning, Edward," said the lawyer. "This is a surprise, I was expecting James."

"I came to ask your advice, Arnold," said Edward. "Me and the boys have had no joy, so far, in our efforts to help James. Would there be any other way for us to help James? To a man we are hoping there is something. We are prepared to take your advice."

"I would most certainly advise against any illegal interference no matter how well meaning. There are too many variables to consider. Should you be exposed, for example, the result would be disastrous for you and most of all for James." Edward was about to speak again, but he stopped when James arrived. "Good to see you, James. I was just telling your cousin here that I was waiting for you. Have you any news for us?" asked the lawyer.

"Hello there, and good to see you both," said James. "I had no luck with Albert, he had a mild stroke last week. But I was able to speak to his nurse. To cut a long story short, she will try to get him to sign the affidavit you gave me, Arnold."

"In that case you must give me the name of the nurse and I will collect the affidavit hoping it has been signed. You should stay local now, James, because of the bail conditions."

Nurse Lilly Brent drew up a chair next to Albert's bed. "How are you feeling this morning, Albert?" she asked.

"Better, thank you, my dear," he replied. Lilly was pleased to hear that his speech, which had been slurred since the stroke, was improving.

"Do you remember Albert, when we spoke the other day, I told you that two young men had asked for you?" When Albert nodded, she continued, telling him about James and his predicament.

"I remember him," said Albert. "A nice young man, on his way to join the army. I had been trying to talk some sense into old Maggie. This, has made me think of something else. I believe it could be her putting flowers for me, on the grave. You see Lilly, she has good days when she takes her medication. Oh dear, oh dear me."

"What is the matter, Albert do you feel ill?" She noticed his breathing had become laboured, and he seemed distressed.

Albert shook his head as he answered, "I'll be all right, give me a minute."

"Very well then," she said slowly. "Settle down and I'll go and get you a nice hot drink. Breakfast will be a while yet."

"Thank you, my dear," he replied. "Don't you go rushing about for me, take your time."

Lewis, wanting to be more involved in James' defence, drove Arnold to the Neath Infirmary. Bryan was at his post when they arrived. Arnold asked if they could possibly see Albert. If not, maybe they could talk to his nurse. "She told me to expect you and I'm to call her when you arrive. Wait here if you please."

Bryan returned within a few minutes. "Nurse Lilly is busy with a patient, so she told me to take you to the waiting room and she won't be long."

They waited for over half an hour before Lilly arrived carrying the envelope, which she handed to Arnold. "Here is your document. I gather you are Mr Owen's lawyer. This has been signed by Albert. Although I have to warn you that his hand is a bit unsteady now. There is another matter, if you have time. I would like to tell you something that I'm sure will be of help to Mr Owen."

Having spent more time than he expected speaking to the nurse, Arnold was impatient to return, knowing he had another client due. So he, and Lewis, made post haste back to the lawyer's office. Once there they found James and the other expected client, waiting to see Arnold. James had to cool his heels, while Arnold saw his client. When the client came out of Arnold's office he left the door wide open and James could see Arnold at his desk. "Come on in, James." called the lawyer. "You see I have the all-important affidavit, and it is signed, by Albert."

"Yes, that's good, what a relief. He signed it this morning then? "James asked.

"I don't know when he signed it, his nurse handed it to me this morning. That as you say is good. Now you can go home. Spend some time with your family, and try to get some rest." Arnold spoke firmly to James. "There is still work for me to do on my opening address and I must speak to our witnesses. Your father-in-law is going to pick up your friend, the vicar, from your village, and he is to stay at Lewis' house for the duration of the trial."

The days before his trial passed agonisingly slowly for James. He had been prepared as much as possible by Arnold. So when the time arrived he was anxious to get it over with.

The monthly sitting of the Swansea County Court was to take place in the Court house of The Guildhall, an imposing building, which houses various council offices and is also the site of horrendous punishments and hangings.

Lewis drove Arnold and James to the Guildhall in his pony and trap. When they arrived Arnold and James went ahead, leaving Lewis to park his vehicle.

The lawyer and his client were to wait in an adjoining room until they were called to court. The waiting room was sparsely furnished, containing just three rows of chairs. Dan, Freddy and two other rough looking characters and a young boy were waiting. There were also two well-dressed, serious looking men, who James assumed were lawyers. Taking the initiative, James avoided eye contact with his former cell mates, and he walked to the back row of chairs. Arnold had no choice but to follow him, although he did acknowledge the two lawyers with a brief good morning. Two constables stood either side of the door, neither of them were known to James.

Five long hours went by during which the waiting room emptied, except for James, and his lawyer. "This is not unusual, James," said the Arnold. "The judge will always keep the most serious cases until last in case of length and possible postponement." If he had not been so nervous James would have laughed when the steward who ushered the accused and their lawyers, came in and out. He was a little man who wore an ill-fitting uniform and a fixed grin. He shuffled in looking at each person in turn with his poppy eyes turning from left to right rapidly. When he called the previous offenders his voice had echoed impatience. However, when he called Arnold and James, his voice took on a more respectful tone, making James think that Arnold must be highly thought of. James looked around the court room in awe. His eyes were immediately drawn to the judge's bench. Behind an impressive oak desk was a large wooden armchair. The back and seat of the chair was upholstered with sage green leather. A beautifully carved wooden structure, as tall as it was broad framed this area. The judge's bench was on a raised platform overlooking the courtroom. Just below that was the well of court, where there was a table for the clerk and the prosecutor sit. To the right of this was a larger table at which all the advocates would sit. Arnold walked in front of

James, guiding him towards the advocates' table. To their right was the jury box and opposite this was the stand where witnesses testify, in full view of the judge, jury and solicitors. Behind the well were the seats for members of the public. Edward, big Dai and his son Billy sat together with some of the mates from work. Behind them sat a row of 'Red Soldiers.' James was amazed to see his former colour sergeant with Rick, Howard, Morg and Gus, all in their smart red coated uniforms! What an impressive sight they made, particularly his former colour sergeant.

"All rise for the honourable Judge Wilfred Harley–Jones," The clerk bellowed, silencing the court.

The portly Judge came into court dragging his left leg behind him. He limped towards his bench, using his left arm to support the offending leg. His deep set eyes showed his surprise when he was confronted with a packed courtroom. Thirty minutes ago, and during his previous cases, the courtroom had been almost empty. He banged his gavel "Order in the court," he roared. The clerk handed the judge two thin sheaves of paperwork, which he glanced through and then placed each one carefully on his desk. "This case has brought with it an amount of notoriety on account of the military interest. I am permitting a representative of the

South Wales Borderers, to record proceedings, and take photographs. There are conditions to my permit. They must not interfere with court procedure or cause disturbance in my court. This being the case, I will inform the court," he paused looking towards the prosecutor, "And that includes the counsellors, that I will not tolerate theatrical displays for the military press. We are ready now. Counsellor Harrison, you may begin."

Rodney Harrison stood, looking with practised severity at the jury. He drew his robe with a flourish, around his tall frame, and walked slowly across the well of the court. When he was as close to the jury as possible he began.

He spoke with exaggerated force, and at length, about the heinous crime against an innocent victim. He continued with a detailed description of a man on his way to his daily labour being attacked and viciously beaten.

After what seemed to be an endless monologue, he closed with the promise of proving the guilt of the defendant.

The judge, who had found it difficult to keep awake during the prosecutor's long speech, was obviously irritated, saying, "Are you ready, counsellor, to begin prosecution?"

"I am, sir," replied the prosecutor, feigning a hurt expression. "I call Mr Dewy Lloyd."

Mr Lloyd, dressed in his finest navy blue suit, and wearing a brightly coloured cravat, made his way to the witness stand. "Mr Lloyd, you were present when the accused made his first attack on the victim during working hours. I require you to explain to the jury exactly what took place," said the pompous prosecutor.

"No, I was not present," replied Mr Lloyd purposefully brief, with the required result. There were gasps and laughter from the public, and the prosecutor turned a deep red. "Surely as their employer, you were called to the scene of the crime sir," said the prosecutor in a confused manner.

"I would not call a clash between two grown men a crime exactly," Mr Lloyd stated. Continuing swiftly he said, "I was not called for, but, I wanted to know what was going on. I had been aware for some time that Tommy Davies was asking for trouble. He was, an aggressive, spiteful, bully. But, he got the work done so I put up with him. That day he went too far and he upset the wrong person."

"Did the defendant attack the deceased?" asked the angry lawyer. "Yes, or no, Mr Lloyd?"

Mr Dewy Lloyd, refusing to be intimidated answered, "I would not call one punch an attack, which is all that James threw at Tommy."

"Your opinion is not called for, sir. Would you therefore, just answer my questions with a simple yes, or no." The lawyer's voice echoed his impatience. "Did you, as a result of his aggressive behaviour, dismiss the defendant?"

"Yes, but…"

"Thank you, Mr Lloyd, that will be all," said the prosecutor, interrupting and dismissing the witness abruptly.

"Do you wish to cross examine the witness, Mr Davies?" asked the judge.

"Yes, your honour," Arnold answered. "Mr Lloyd. You have described the victim as an aggressive, spiteful, bully. Therefore, he must have made enemies, who would seek vengeance." Arnold paused to give the witness time for thought. Mr Lloyd, nodding in agreement, was about to speak when Arnold continued. "That being so, may we believe that one or more men would be capable of a vicious attack on him?"

"Objection," called the prosecutor. "Supposition, and leading the witness."

"Sustained," said the judge. "You will refrain from leading the witness, counsellor."

"Yes, my lord," Arnold replied. "Mr Lloyd, are there any incidents that you know of, involving aggressive behaviour by the deceased, which may have caused retaliation of this villainous nature."

"Yes indeed, too many. He was always upsetting somebody. I could name quite a few. But that would be what your friend over there would call supposition," Mr Lloyd replied, pointing towards the prosecutor.

'*Clever man*' thought Arnold as he said, "Thank you, Mr Lloyd, that will be all."

Arnold returned to his seat. The prosecutor called three more witnesses one following the other. James recognised them as being the drinking partners of Tommy Davies, from the Farmers Arms. Each of them painted a different picture of Tommy than the one that had been described by Mr Lloyd. They praised Tommy Davies as a good friend and an honest hard worker! Arnold did not cross-examine these witnesses.

"I call Mrs Davies to the stand, if it pleases your honour," announced the prosecutor with a flourish of his robe.

Tommy's mother took the stand.

With the exception of her peroxide hair, which was almost covered by a hat, she had the appearance of a respectable middle-aged woman. Her mode of dress was plain and she wore no facial make up. "Mrs Davies, before I begin I want you to know you have my deepest sympathy, for your loss." The prosecutor looked from the witness to the jury. "Nevertheless, I must ask you, to tell the court what time your son left home on the day he was brutally attacked."

"He left the same time he always did, half past six. He always went early 'cos he liked to 'ave a cup of char, before he started work at half past seven. Hard worker he was, my boy. Looked after me he has, ever since his father done a bunk." She began to cry, speaking through tears she sobbed "Now I got nobody and nothing."

"Thank you, Mrs Davies. You have been very brave. I have no further questions for this witness my lord," and the prosecutor returned to his seat.

"Re-direction counsellor?" the judge asked looking at Arnold.

"Yes, if you please, my lord," Arnold paused, waiting for the witness to wipe her eyes and blow her nose. "Mrs Davies, you have stated that your son 'looked after you'. Are we to believe that was financially, or physically, because you are not in full-time employment, and you appear to be in good health. Therefore, I assume he supported you financially, is that so?"

"You mean I haven't got a job. Well no." She had stopped crying and had taken on a defensive stance, "But I looked after the house and the food for my boy, and I saw to it that his washing was done nice for him."

"Thank you, Mrs. Davies, that will be all. I have no further questions for this witness, my lord."

Returning to his seat, Arnold saw that James was pale, and looked anxious. "Don't worry James," he whispered. "I know you think that the jury sympathise with her, but there is a twist to come."

'Oh my god, I'm worried all right.' thought James. *'I feel sorry for her, so the jury have got to be sympathetic.'*

"Counsellor Harrison?" the judge addressed the prosecutor questioning his failure to move.

"I beg your pardon, my lord. I rest my case."

"At this late time of the day I will call a recess until nine o'clock tomorrow morning." Once more the gavel came down with a bang.

Outside the courtroom James was surrounded by friends and family. His father, who had been sitting in the corridor with Reverend Richards was first to reach him.

"James, my boy, how are you holding up?" David held his son in a bear hug. "They didn't call upon our good vicar, so he said that would mean another day tomorrow."

"Yes, Dad," James answered his father. "I hope that's all right with you and Reverend Richards?"

"Certainly is James, we will do whatever we can to help you." The vicar shook James' hand as he spoke.

"Dad, I must be causing Mama so much worry, I only hope it's not making her ill. She's had enough worry over me, when I was in the army. How is she Dad?" James asked.

"Don't be fretting now about Mama. She's so sure of your innocence, that she and tells us all you'll be home in no time," his father answered.

James was then confronted by his mates from work and they were followed by his comrades from the army. All of them, wishing him well and confident of his innocence.

The following morning when James entered the court he looked around the public seats. He was nodding towards his friends when his eyes came to rest on someone sitting in the front row. Lilly returned his gaze with a sweet smile, Arnold saw James' look of surprise. He placed a hand on James' shoulder and whispered, "Sit down, James, I will explain later."

"All rise for the court," bellowed the clerk.

"Taking his seat, the judge began by addressing Arnold. "Counsellor Dawson, I hope you are ready put your case for the defence."

Arnold rose, and began his opening address by describing his client as a decent family man, defending the honour of his wife. He referred to James' heroism as a soldier who fought with comrades against impossible odds. In an effort to keep his address as brief as possible, he ended with the assurance of his client's innocence and his own ability to provide the necessary proof.

First to be called for the defence was big Dai. "I call Mr David Bates to the stand." Arnold began by questioning him about the conflict between James and Tommy Davies.

Big Dai spoke clearly, even though he was nervous. He was determined to keep cool and do his best for his friend. "As you say, sir, I saw and heard what happened that day. Tommy insulted James' wife, which was well out of order. I don't want to speak ill of the dead, but in the case of Tommy Davies, I don't mind telling you that he was a nasty piece of work. The way he spoke was enough to get any man mad, so any one of us would have taken a poke at him, and that's all James did, sir."

"Thank you, Mr Bates, that is all from me."

"Re-direct counsellor?" the judge asked the prosecutor.

"Do you know of anyone, other than the accused, who has attacked, and knocked the victim unconscious? And you will just answer yes, or no."

Big Dai had no choice he answered, "No."

"I have finished with this witness, my lord" said the prosecutor aggressively.

James' colour sergeant was next to take the stand. He spoke of the bravery shown by James in the face of the enemy. He told of the battles during which James had shown such courage, describing James as an honourable man, and one of a company of men, who he was proud to be associated with.

"Were you surprised, sergeant, to hear that James has been accused of murder?" Arnold asked.

"I was shocked, sir," he replied. "When you live with men, under such severe conditions, you get to know each other like family. And, I pride myself on knowing every one of my boys as if they were my own. So I can say in all honesty, that in my opinion, James Owen would not have committed the cowardly act he is accused of."

"Thank you, sir. That is all from me for now," said Arnold.

"Do you wish to cross question the witness, counsellor?" the judge said to the prosecutor.

"Just one question, my lord," was the reply. "Were you present during the crime, sergeant?"

"No, of course not," replied the sergeant.

"In that case, I suggest the witness be excused your honour."

"Counsellor, Mr Dawson, you may proceed," the judge said to Arnold.

"Yes, your honour. I call Constable Sidney Brown.

Sidney, wearing his smart uniform, and carrying his policeman's hat, took the stand.

"Constable Brown, am I right in saying that the deceased and his mother are known to you?" asked Arnold.

"Yes, you are right, sir, I have arrested Mrs Davies several times for prostitution. I also saw her quite often at the station when other officers had arrested her. The deceased came to the station at least once, to my knowledge, to pay her fine, when his mother had no money. At the time she was almost hysterical. She shouted at the constable saying that he hadn't given her time to earn enough to pay her fine."

There was laughter and exclamations from the public seats.

Bang went the judge's gavel. "Order, order, I will have order in my court."

"Thank you, constable, that will be all." Arnold glanced at the prosecutor, who remained in his seat, looking dejected.

Next to take the stand was the Reverend Thomas Richards.

"Reverend Richards, how long have you known the accused?"

"James regularly attended my church with his parents and siblings from birth. However, I was formally introduced to the young James when his parents brought him to my humble church school. He was then ten years of age." The vicar paused. "He proved to be an exceptional scholar. By the age of thirteen years he was employed as my assistant, teaching the younger scholars to read and write. Later, when he attained the age of sixteen, he left home, to find more lucrative employment in Swansea. James returned regularly to visit his parents and also your humble servant. During his service as a soldier in her majesty's army, James wrote home as often as he could. It is my sincere opinion this is not a young man, who would, under any circumstances, commit such a sinful crime."

"Thank you, Reverend Richards." *'What an orator!'* thought Arnold.

"Re-direct counsellor?" asked the judge.

"Just one question, my lord," answered the prosecutor. "Were you present during the attack on the victim, sir?"

"I did not have to be…" the vicar began when he was rudely interrupted by the prosecutor.

"That will be all. No more questions from me," he said impatiently.

"Thank you, your reverence, please resume your seat." said Judge Harley-Jones. And he glared at the prosecutor. Then he turned to Arnold. "You may call your next witness, counsellor."

"In order to resume your honour, if I may at first refer you to the affidavit signed by one Albert Morris, a retired police sergeant. My next witness will corroborate the affidavit, signed by him. I call, Miss Margaret Gibbs to the stand."

James was shocked when he saw the smartly dressed old lady, who sat next to Lilly, rise and take the stand.

"Miss Gibbs, did you witness the presence of the defendant at the Neath cemetery on the seventh of December eighteen hundred and seventy six, at seven thirty a.m.?"

"Yes, sir, I did" she squeaked.

James almost fell off his chair. He would recognise that squeaky voice anywhere! But this could not be the same crazy old woman, he remembered from that day with Albert!

"Thank you very much, Miss Gibbs," said a delighted Arnold.

"Cross examination, Mr Harrison?" asked the judge raising his eyebrows.

"May I ask, Madam, how you can be sure of the time the defendant arrived at the cemetery?" the lawyer enquired.

"You may. And I'm Miss, not Madam." Squeaky voice or not, she spoke with authority, and had her answers ready. "Albert is very proud of his retirement pocket watch, which keeps perfect time.

So he knows when it is seven thirty. That's the time we go to the cemetery every morning, and he always calls for me first, at seven twenty."

"I have no more questions for this witness, your honour," said the disgruntled prosecutor, returning to his seat once more.

"Thank you, Miss Davies, you may return to your seat," the judge said politely.

"As there are no further witness to be called, we will recess until nine o'clock tomorrow morning," the judge announced. "When both counsellors will be ready with their summations." And bang went the gavel.

Nurse Lilly and Maggie were talking to Lewis outside the courthouse when James and Arnold appeared. Lilly was beaming and even old Maggie managed a smile.

Arnold caught James' arm and held him back. "Just thank them for now, James, and I will reveal all to you later." He said in a low voice.

Doing as he was bid James walked up to the two women and took each one by the hand. "Thank you so much," he said unable to hide a look of amazement at Maggie. "You and Albert have, no doubt, saved my life today. I am lost for the right words to express my gratitude."

"We are both glad to help you, James," said the lovely Lilly. "Albert sent his best wishes to you and he hopes to see you when he is better. I have good friends in Swansea, where Maggie and I are going to spend the night. We want to be here, and see your acquittal tomorrow."

Maggie had remained silent, but she had held on to James' hand, which he lightly squeezed, saying, "You look beautiful today, my friend."

This brought about an unexpected reaction from Maggie. Tears came into her eyes, and she hugged him, placing both arms around his waist.

Lilly took Maggie gently by her shoulder saying, "Time to go now, Maggie dear. I see our friends have arrived with their buggy."

They went, leaving James more perplexed than ever.

"Come on, boys," said Lewis to James and his lawyer. "Back to my house, with the good vicar and me. Emma will be there already, James, waiting with Edith."

"Thank you for the offer, Lewis," said Arnold. "But I must decline, there is still work to be done on my closing summation for tomorrow. Lewis is well aware of all the pertinent facts, James. He will be able to reveal all as well as I. See you both tomorrow at nine sharp."

Back at the Lewis residence James and his father-in-law, embraced their wives before Lewis ushered them into his comfortable lounge.

"I would say, James, that your first surprise today was the testimony of the young constable, Sidney Brown," Lewis said.

"Yes, indeed," James replied. "What brought that about?"

Lewis smiled at James who was sitting opposite him and vicar Richards, each of them on a matching armchair. They were drinking their tea and eating the sandwiches Edith and Emma had brought in to them. The ladies were sitting quietly on the chaise lounge next to the bay window.

"Sidney arrived at Arnold's office yesterday evening, offering to testify for you. He was aware of the damage done to your defence by the testimony of Tommy's mother. And when Sid exposed her true colours to him, Arnold gladly accepted his offer."

"That was good of him," James interjected.

"Yes, but, your biggest shock must have been the appearance of Miss Margaret Gibbs."

"Too right, Lewis, I almost fell off my chair when I recognised Maggie, and saw nurse Lilly. If it wasn't for her voice, I would never have known that smart old lady was the same old crone from the cemetery," said James.

"Well relax, and sit tight because I have quite a tale to relate about poor Maggie." Lewis paused to finish his sandwich and drink his tea.

"Maggie was forty two years of age, living with her parents and resigned to spinsterhood, when she met a man. He was a ship's captain whose ship was docked in Swansea. Maggie met him when mutual friends introduced them. It was love at first sight, and they spent two glorious months of courtship. A whirlwind romance, you might say. Before he returned to his ship he proposed marriage, and bought Maggie an engagement ring. They wrote to each other and Maggie still has his precious love letters."

"Almost a year later, Maggie was informed of his death. He died on a tropical island, as a result of being bitten by a venomous snake. His will was found in his cabin, and he had named Maggie as his next of kin and his sole heir. His body was brought home, and Maggie buried him in the cemetery, where Albert later buried his family."

James was listening intently when Lewis stopped once more. "Now, James, before I continue, we will have a glass of wine." James taking the wine tried to hide his impatience, until Lewis continued.

"Maggie was inconsolable and she was overwhelmed with grief. When she returned from the burial she ran to her bedroom and began to scream. She wailed and screamed all that day and through the night. As a result she damaged her vocal chords, which caused the impediment in her speech." Lewis paused to take a sip of wine.

"When her parents died soon after, she became something of an eccentric recluse. The only person who she would associate with was Albert's wife, Gertrude, they had been friends since childhood, and Maggie trusted the kind gentlewoman. Gertrude would coax Maggie to take the laudanum that her doctor had advised — small doses worked to calm her. When she was calm Gertrude would get her to bathe, wash her hair and put clean clothes on. When Gertrude and his sons died Albert took on the role, as best he could, of helper to Maggie. When Albert had an accident and was taken to the infirmary, Maggie reverted to her old ways. She became depressed, and stopped caring for herself. But, she still went every day to the grave of her dead lover. This was where Albert told his nurse to find Maggie, coax her in Albert's name, to take a few drops of the laudanum. Lilly should ask her to testify for James, and then help her to bathe and dress smartly. Albert knew that Maggie had a wardrobe full of fine clothes, and plenty of money." Lewis stopped for breath.

"There is more to this tale, James, but I think I have covered the main facts for you."

"Oh my God, Lewis, that is such an incredible story. Poor Maggie, and what a good man Albert is.

Then there's the kindness of Lilly — what friends to have, and they hardly know me!"

"Albert must have been impressed with you, James, and Maggie obviously has complete faith in his judgement. With his affidavit and Maggie's testimony, you have your alibi. There is also the testimony of the constable which will discredit Tommy's mother, and deny her the sympathy of the jury. So you, James, and you, my dear Emma, must take heart and each of you show a brave face tomorrow."

"Arnold did tell me that we had presented a good case," James said. "However, the prosecutor in his summation, will do his damnedest to achieve a guilty verdict. And we do not know what he has prepared. Although we are more than hopeful, it's not over yet. That being so, my darling," he held Emma's hand as he looked into her eyes, "I need you to be brave whatever happens. And I pray that I will come through that door and take you in my arms again."

"All right, James, I will do as you ask," said his wife. "But in my heart I know that you will be found innocent."

There was a crowd of people outside the courtroom when James and Arnold arrived. There was no room left inside, the seats were all occupied and people were standing at the back and in the aisles.

The constables were attempting to turf out the overflow in the central aisle, as James and Arnold battled their way to through.

With great difficulty the constables completed their task, until there was at least one aisle clear. When the constables returned to their posts, the clerk stood and announced the arrival of the Judge.

"All rise for the court."

The Honourable Judge Wilfred Harley-Jones entered. He scrutinized the public area and frowned when he saw how many people were standing at the back and sides of the courtroom.

"Due to the overcrowded situation, I assume there are those who have come to my court for the first time. Everyone will be aware, that order will be kept in my court, at all times."

To reinforce his point, bang went the gavel.

"Counsellor for the prosecution, you will begin your summation."

"Thank you, my lord," said Rodney Harrison.

"Ladies and gentlemen of the jury, you have heard conflicting opinions of the victim from witnesses," the lawyer said with an expression of disbelief on his face. "Who are you to believe?" He paused, raising his eyebrows. "Witnesses produced by the defence, who were merely acquainted with the victim, or his mother, and friends, who knew him intimately?"

Harrison spent ten minutes describing the hard working young man in glowing terms. Then a further ten minutes was spent recounting the attack, how the victim had been set upon, battered and viciously murdered.

"The way that the mother of the victim was exposed to her detriment was cruel," Harrison said angrily. He then changed, into a sympathetic, kind man. "This mother was destitute when her husband left her with a child to support. She was forced to earn a crust in a manner, which, if she had a choice, she would have avoided."

Once again he abruptly changed, this time becoming the studious lawyer. "And as to the so called alibi of the accused, the witness, an old woman, relied on an old man to know the time of day. Either could have been mistaken. Elderly people do make such errors. We have also been informed, that the said old man is unwell, too ill in fact, to come to court." Harrison broke off, allowing the jury a few seconds to evaluate his supposition.

"You have heard how the accused acted as a soldier. We know he killed many men, therefore we know that he is capable of extreme violence." Emphasising the word killed, he carried straight on.

"Members of the jury, it is for you to decide. Did this man kill Tommy Davies? Did he seek vengeance on the man he hated? I submit that there is only one possible verdict to be arrived at. That must be, 'Guilty as charged."

"I rest my case, my lord," said Prosecutor Harrison returning to his seat.

'Oh my God, Arnold was right when he said it was not over yet,' James thought.

"Thank you counsellor," said the judge, much relieved that the prosecutor had kept the length of his summation to within the required hour.

"We are ready for your summation for the defence, Counsellor Dawson."

"Thank you, your honour," James's lawyer strode towards the jury as he spoke.

"Ladies and gentlemen of the jury, my learned friend has informed the court that my client killed many men. Isn't that what soldiers are expected do, when they face the enemies of our country?" Arnold paused with a suggestion of a smirk on his lips. Then he became deadly serious. "His actions as a soldier, were praised and rewarded by Her Majesty, Queen Victoria. He wears his medal with pride, and so he should. Did my learned friend mean to infer, that the actions of our brave soldiers could be groundwork for murderers? I hope not, because the lives of us all are in their hands, when we are threatened."

As expected, the prosecutor glared at Arnold.

"Mr Albert Morris, previously referred to as 'the old man', by my learned friend..." Arnold turned his gaze from the jury to the prosecutor and back again. "Mr Morris, a retired police officer, is a respected member of his community. His illness was referred to. In fact, Mr Morris had an accident which resulted in a broken leg, and this occurred more than two years after his meeting with my client. You may therefore be assured that Mr Morris was in good health, both physically and mentally, on the fateful day. And Miss Margaret Gibbs, spoken of as 'the old woman', I am sure she satisfied the court of her acute awareness, without help from me. Therefore we have proved that my client was miles away from the scene of the crime." He ended with, "I will not tire you by prolonging my summation further.

Suffice it to say, ladies and gentlemen of the jury, you hold this brave man's life in your hands. You have the power to bring in the innocent verdict, and by doing so, you will ensure that justice be done."

There followed a buzz in the court which was curtailed by the Judge.

"Order, order in the court," Bang, bang and yet another bang came from the judge's gavel.

"Ladies and gentlemen of the jury, you will retire to the jury room, escorted by the clerk and a guard." "The court will take a recess while the jury deliberate."

James looked towards his lawyer. "I'm almost afraid to ask, Arnold."

"Don't be, James. We have done all we can, which I am confident was enough."

Unfortunately James could not share his lawyer's confidence. "The jury could sympathise with Tommy's family and friends. Do we have to stay here, Arnold, while we wait?" James asked.

"Afraid so, James, and it could be for quite a while."

The jury returned within two hours, and the clerk, immediately after, called out, "All rise for the Honourable Judge Harley-Jones."

"Ladies and gentlemen of the jury, have you reached a verdict?" asked the Judge.

The foreman rose. "We have, my lord. We find the accused innocent of all charges."

When he uttered the word 'innocent', numerous voices shouted, 'YES!'

The judge banged his gavel with a vengeance. "Order, I say order! Thank you, Mr Foreman. The jury is dismissed. Mr Owen, you are free to go," said the judge, who was anxious to leave.

Emma, helped through the crowd by her father, was the first to reach her husband. But they were soon joined by David and Anne and then friends.

James introduced Maggie and Lilly to his wife. Emma thanked them both, and asked if they would join in the celebrations at her father's house.

"Thank you for the kind offer, but our friends wait for us, we promised to spend tonight with them. We both stayed to congratulate James on his acquittal and to give you both our best wishes," she said happily.

Emma and James hugged them both, promising to keep in touch.

"This time, I'll have no excuses," said Lewis. "You're all coming back with me to celebrate James' acquittal."

Anne and David declined as they wanted to get home to their little ones who were being looked after by Aunt Martha. Anne hugged her son with tears of joy in her eyes, as she and David said goodbye.

Lewis and Edith's house was soon full, and their garden took the overflow. The celebrations began at five thirty and went on until after midnight.

James and Emma's children were put to bed in their grandparents' house. Much later, James and his lovely wife walked home, hand in hand.

"That's it then, my beautiful girl. No more worries, we can get on with our lives in peace."

Chapter 11
1938

The Zulu warrior roared a war cry, as young Billy Hopkins slithered from the Heathens' blood soaked assegai. This blood curdling cry echoed in James' ears with ominous regularity. However, news of the Tattoo may have caused his nightmare to return last night. For the past few days, his thoughts had been of meeting his comrades, and taking part in the Military Tattoo.

When he eventually awoke, James was awash with perspiration. He tried but could not stop, the cries of the injured and dying men, which continued to fill his ears. Nor could he suppress the sickening feeling from the stench of blood, seeping through his nostrils.

In spite of his advanced years, his brain was still extremely active. He could visualise, with perfect accuracy, the grotesque scene of carnage that he had witnessed on that fateful day.

He drew himself up and sat on the edge of his bed, covering his face with his hands, he fought to recover his composure.

Several minutes later his hands had stopped shaking, and he was calm enough to open his left eye. He stretched a hand out to the chest of drawers beside his bed. There were two containers and a glass of water on the unit. He picked up the largest tin and took out a set of false teeth. He shook off the cleaning powder and dipped the teeth into the water before putting them into his mouth. Then he reached for the small round tin, opened it, and took out his glass eye. Lifting his right eye lid with his free hand, he put the glass eye in place. These actions were habitual; it did not matter how he felt, James would not stir from his bed, until he was equipped with teeth and 'both' eyes.

Despite constant denials of personal vanity, he spent great deal of time and effort on his appearance. To totally avoid the inevitable deterioration which came with age, had of course been impossible. However, all through his adult life, James had attempted to preserve his lithe and muscular body. He was accustomed to taking brisk walks daily — paying very little regard to the weather, except to dress accordingly. Unlike many elderly men, of over six feet in height, James had also remained erect in posture.

His hair had turned white overnight during the Battle of Rorke's Drift. At the time he was so grateful to be alive, that this oddity did not cause him undue concern. In point of fact, some said that his white hair was not only distinguished, but extremely attractive. Fortunately, his hair had remained abundant, and he kept it well groomed, along with his 'military moustache'.

With the exception of his glass eye, which was really only noticeable when he was tired, James could be described as being a handsome, elderly man. His daughter-in-law, Lottie often described him thus.

It was Lottie who had persuaded him to come and live with her and his son, David Lewis, when his darling Emma died.

James walked over to the long glass door which led to the back yard, and drew back the curtain. As there were no windows in his room, this was his single source of daylight. He strode back across the room to the other wooden door, this one opened on to a passage. He took down his thick over coat, which was kept on a hook his side of the door, and slipped it around his shoulders.

As the welcome daylight shone in, James sighed, and slumped into his aged leather armchair. He gazed absently around his room; there was the old three mirror dressing table, which was really a female's item, but precious to him. He could imagine his lovely wife, Emma, sitting there, taking out her hair pins and releasing her beautiful black tresses.

He had loved to watch her brushing her hair until it gleamed and flowed over her shoulders, down to her little waist. Sometimes he could swear she was still alive and sitting there, his day dreams were so realistic.

Placed on the dressing table was a photograph. He saw himself with Gus, Howard, Rick and Gwyn. They were all standing, posing proudly in their new army uniforms. This made James smile. It reminded him of their first day, when Gus had a wind problem — he caused such a stink in the attesting line — it made the soldier giving out the uniforms go berserk. That was when James first thought, maybe this was where the saying, 'swear like a trooper' began.

Above the dressing table, hanging on the wall, opposite his chair, were the Ox horns, the Zulu shield and the assegai.

Once again, his thoughts flashed back to the source of his nightmares. He remembered the scene of devastation that followed after the battle of Rorkes Drift. Dead bodies by the hundreds, lay in tiers alongside the mealy bag ramparts below him, and more bodies, mostly those of Zulu warriors, lay scattered throughout the camp.

He tried to focus on the occasional dead soldiers, saying a silent prayer for them. "Only the good die young," he moaned, "that phrase could well have originated back then. In order to survive that lot, a man had to shut the gates of mercy, and become a relentless, murdering devil. He had to be harder and more ruthless, than the swarms of bloodthirsty Zulus bearing down on him."

He continued to murmur to himself. "Washing their spears, that's what they called it, when they dug the sharp point into a man's body, and tore out half his innards. It was a case of kill or be killed. Well I killed, God forgive me, so many men that day. But I survived, and sixty odd years later I'm still here to tell the tale."

He became calmer and looking upwards he gave a slight smile, and said quietly. "I wouldn't mind a few more years as well, that's if it suits your plans. But if not then I can't complain, for I've certainly had a long run, some good and some the worst." He paused, taking a deep breath. "But some of it has been downright marvelous."

His gaze wondered downwards over the mantle shelf then came to an abrupt halt at the fire grate which made his thoughts returned to the present. "That's enough of this time wasting now James, you should clear out the ashes before Lottie comes in." He muttered to himself, as he made his way across the room and began his task.

With a heavy sigh, James proceeded to clean up the grate. Having removed the ashes, he re-laid the fire. "That's one less job for her." He said, feeling pleased with his self. "Now I'll put a match to it and put the guard up, while I take the ashes out."

Just a few minutes later, James was carrying the bowl of ashes out to the back yard. He emptied the bowl on to the cinder path, treading in the new ashes to cover the old. He then made his way to the lavatory, which was housed in a stone made 'lean to', built on to the back wall of the house, facing the small garden.

By the time he arrived back in his room, the fire was burning brightly. He noticed that Lottie had been in, changed his sheets, pillow slips and left a clean shirt on his bed. A jug of hot water, a bowl, a cake of soap and a flannel, were on the chest of draws, together with clean towel. He bolted the door before stripping down for an all over wash.

Having completed his ablutions, he dressed and sat back once again on his arm chair. He was quite content to sit awhile in his pleasant, comfortable bed sitting room. His thoughts were of meeting his comrades — Rick and Gus would be there. Howard will be missing this time. He had died of a heart attack, in the arms of his beautiful wife, two years ago.

James had kept in touch, by mail, with his mates. He also met Hywel occasionally when he was visiting his family in Llanboidy.

Hywel had written to James, a week ago, concerning their part in the re-enactment of the battle at Rorke's Drift. He was looking forward to the Tattoo, but he expressed deep anxiety about appearing in front of a huge audience and members of the press. Nevertheless, he promised to be on the early train, which stopped at Swansea. He hoped that he and James could travel together to Gateshead.

James was disturbed from his reverie by the arrival of his granddaughter, Edna. She knocked on his door calling, "Only me, Gramps, can I come in?"

"Yes, Edna, come on in, my dear."

"I brought your clothes for tomorrow. I steamed and pressed your Sunday best suit, washed and ironed your best white shirt, and your black socks. Mammy Lottie said she has seen to your underwear, a few handkerchiefs, also your white collars and studs."

"Thank you, Edna love, you girls are so good to me. If you hang my suit behind the door, I will sort the rest. I have my bag ready to pack. The toiletries will go in tomorrow morning, when I have finished using my shaving soap, scissors, and other things I may need tonight."

"What about my young Tony, coming after school, Gramps? Shall I tell him not to disturb you today?"

"No need, Edna love, I do enjoy his visits. But I will send him home earlier than usual, so that I can take a bath and be ready for tomorrow."

"And there's tonight, shall I tell Ralph that you'll be giving the pub a miss then, Gramps?"

"Oh yes, I don't want to have a hangover tomorrow." He said with a grin. "Right you are. I'm off, bye for now, see you later."

Most evenings James' son, David, and Edna's husband, Ralph, would visit the Rhydings Hotel. Referred to by the men as 'the Brynmill local, 'the pub' or simply 'over the road.' They enjoyed a pint of Welsh bitter and an hour of relaxation, with big Dai and their mates, before their evening meal. Once invited, James readily joined in this regular treat.

Lottie accepted this habit without comment, except for one evening, just a day after James moved in. James was sitting in the kitchen; he was talking to Lottie while she was preparing the evening meal, when they heard the creak of the garden gate. "Here he comes," said Lottie, "now watch this."

Making a good job of imitating David, she walked towards James stroking imaginary perspiration from her brow. "I've had hard day today in that boiler room. I think I'll wash and go for a pint before dinner, love. Coming over the road for a quickie, Dad?"

They both laughed together until Lottie put a finger to her mouth. "Hush now, here he comes."

David came through the back door, behaving just as Lottie had prophesied. Before he had chance to complete his short speech, he was interrupted, by a burst of laughter from James and chuckles from Lottie. He looked from one to the other, nonplused "What the hell is going on with you two?" he asked. Lottie, still chuckling, simply returned to her chores.

"Go on and get yourself cleaned up, me and Lottie were just sharing a private joke." James replied, grinning.

James looked back on this period in his life and on the years that had followed with satisfaction. They had been good years spent with David, Lottie and the family. Although Lottie was his daughter-in-law, James loved her as much, if not more, than his own children. Everyone loved Lottie; David still adored her after nearly fifty years of marriage, eleven children and those countless grandchildren.

'Born and bred a lady,' thought James, 'but she had readily adapted to her reduced circumstances, without complaint, for love of my son, David.'

As the daughter of a wealthy publican, Charlotte (Lottie) Jane Dowman, had been 'born into money'. Old Dowman, as they all called Lottie's father, had doted on his three daughters. From birth, they had been showered with every luxury. When they were old enough, they had been educated in Dumbarton, the most exclusive private school in Swansea.

Old Dowman was consumed with fury when Lottie ran off, to marry David Owen. Because David was a lowly plumber, who worked in the local hospital, her father had 'cut her off', as if she had died.

Her sisters had kept in touch with her, and were good to her, until Agnes, her youngest sister, eloped with their coachman!

Grace, the elder of the three, was not blessed with her siblings' beauty. Her mousy coloured hair, large nose and tall thick body were 'gifts' from her father. Her sisters, Lottie and Agnes, had inherited their mothers beauty, both slim and petite, with abundant dark blonde hair and deep blue eyes.

Grace adored her sisters and had been particularly generous to Lottie, without her father's knowledge and sometimes without David's knowledge. Whilst he did not mind gifts for the house or the children, David was too proud to accept financial help from her family.

The silence in his room was curtailed by the sounds of breakfast being prepared in the kitchen, followed by Lottie's slow footsteps approaching through the passage.

She came into his room carrying a tray of porridge, toast and a mug of steaming tea. He felt a wave of anger as he watched her take small painful steps towards him, then he looked at her lovely face and the anger was replaced by an overwhelming sadness.

"I could have come out to have that, Lottie, you should try and rest those legs more." He said as he took the proffered tray and rested it on his lap.

Lottie always knew when James was upset, his strong welsh accent became even more pronounced. "Now James, you know I like you to stay in here 'til Edna's lot have gone to school." As Lottie replied, she smiled, softening the effects of her reprimand.

"Eat up your breakfast, James. I'll let young Tony come in for five minutes, but do not start your story telling, he'll only be late for school again."

The last few words were spoken as she made for the door.

"That pretty smile doesn't fool me for one minute, my girl. I know those legs are killing you." He said, wagging a finger at her. "Why don't you take a break, just now and then, my dear?" He added gently.

She smiled again and nodded her head as she closed the door. He knew that she had already dismissed his advice, and was thinking about her next chore.

'I'm sure I know why she uses that lily of the valley scent stuff. I think it is to cover up another smell. One I recognise from years ago, and then they called it gangrene.'

James' thoughts were interrupted; his great grandson, Tony, came bounding in through the door, then leaping on to the bed.

"Granny Lottie said I could come in for a minute, but I mustn't be late for school. If I come after school, will you read me an adventure from your books Gramps?" Tony blurted out.

"Hold on boy, hold on will you, stop for breath a minute." James laughed, delighted by the boy's enthusiasm and energy. In a more serious tone he added, "You get to school on time, and learn your lessons well. Pay special attention to the reading and writing, boy. These are not ordinary books in here, you know." he added, pointing to the diaries on the chest. "They are diaries — recording all my adventures and if I had not learned to write, well then, we wouldn't be able to read them now, would we?"

The child looked hard at the old man, his dark eyes widening. "Did you do all that writing by yourself, Gramps?" he asked.

"Yes, boy, all by myself. Now get to school, before we both cop it from your Granny Lottie and your mammy."

Tony laughed contemptuously at the thought of anyone, even his mammy, daring to stand up to 'Grandpa with the white hair'. He jumped down off the bed and made for the door calling "See you after school then for a story."

Tony returned later as promised. "Here I am then, Gramps, ready for a good story."

James smiled and took out one of his diaries. "These stories are between you and me, boy. Don't forget, your mammy and granny will not like some of what I have written, or some of the things I have done." He opened the diary and began reading.

Today we were given instruction. With the new, absolutely fantastic Martini Henri; just holding it makes a man feel ten feet tall. The power of this rifle in volley firing is unbelievable.

My new comrades, David Jones, Howard Brown, David Morgan, Gwynnfor Lloyd, and David Llewellyn from the Swansea Valleys, all arrived about the same time as me. We got together for our dinner tonight, and talked of nothing but these new rifles.

James stopped reading and pointed to the photograph of the soldiers. "This is me, Tony, with my mates, holding our Martini-Henry rifles."

"It's a very big gun, Gramps," said the wide eyed boy. "Do all soldiers get one when they join the army?"

"Yes, they do, boy."

They talked for a while. Tony wanted to know more about the rifle and so James gave him a more detailed description of the rifle and dealt with the boy's interruptions patiently.

James took out another one of his diaries. He leafed through the pages, trying to find a suitable extract to read to the boy.

"Right, Tony, this about when I got to South Africa."

We docked today at East London. The reefs here were impossible to negotiate so we were taken ashore on serf boats.

Tony, with the inevitable interruption, asked, "What's a serf boat Gramps? And what's a reef?"

"Well now, these serf boats were like flat bottomed rowing boats, Tony. Don't forget, this was sixty odd years ago, we didn't have any of your modern engine driven boats. As for reefs, well they can be big mounds of sand, or rocks, in the sea or towards the surface, hindering the passage of big boats and ships." James thought for a second, then decided to make his story telling more interesting for the boy. "There have been many shipwrecks caused by dangerous reefs. You see boy, if the bottom of a ship was to hit a rock, then it would split open. The sea would then gush through the hole — the ship would sink and all the people would end up in the sea."

"I'm glad that never happened to your ship, Gramps," said Tony seriously, "but anyway — you would be all right, because you're an amazing, strong swimmer."

"Yes — well your Dad told me that you're pretty good in the water, Tony, so you should be all right too. And by the time you're a man, you will be as strong in the water as me. You're lucky to be living at the seaside." James replied. "Shall I read a bit more now, before you have to go home?"

When Tony nodded eagerly, James continued.

C and B company were the first to be taken ashore, and by the end of the day more than eight hundred men were landed. Then we left, by train, for King Williams Town. One of the boys had a pack of cards, so we passed the time playing card games and eating the last of our rations.

"Will you teach me to play cards properly, Gramps?" Once again, Tony interrupted James. "I can only play snap, and that's all right, but I would like to be able to play proper card games, like the men."

"Right then," James replied, "What do you want to do now, more reading or play cards?"

Tony was silent for a moment. "Will you just tell me about the train first? Did it blow loads of smoke, like the one my Dad took me to see in the Swansea station? Or was it like one of the trams, in town?" he asked. "And then we can play cards after if you like." He added.

"If that's what you'd like, then I will tell you about the train," said James, "but we will not have time for more tonight. It will soon be time for me to have my bath."

"That will be all right, Gramps."

"It was only similar to the Swansea train in that it was coal fuelled. That means there was a fire in the engine car, which was kept going by the driver's mate, who would keep shoveling coal on the fire.

"The carriages were not sufficient to carry all these soldiers, and so the rest of us were packed into trailers. These were like long wooden boxes on wheels, with benches for us to sit on."

James took a deep breath and changed the tone of his voice to sound severe. "There were more trailers spaced out along the train, these carried the big guns, cannons and the pride of the army, the Gatling gun. The gunners and their ammunition rode with the big guns. They were being transported and also, we had to be prepared for attacks along the way. And this is how we travelled to our first military post in Africa."

"Did you ever get to fire one of those big guns, Gramps?" Tony asked.

"Not me Tony. For this I am thankful, because those men very rarely survived a battle. I think that's enough war talk now, because I have to send you home. We can play cards another time."

The following day, James rose early. He washed and dressed, taking more care than usual on his appearance. However, he was ready to go when Lottie knocked his door.

"Tea and toast in the kitchen, Dad." She called through the door.

"I will be right there, Lottie." He replied.

James finished his breakfast hurriedly, wanting to make an early start.

"I will not hold you back, Dad, I know you're in a hurry to meet up with your friends before the meeting."

"I am looking forward to catching up with my old mates again. Though there are not that many of us left now." James ended with a sigh.

"Well you're still with us, thanks be to God," she said with feeling, "Now, off you go, it is almost six a.m., you do not want to miss your train. I hope you have the best of times, Dad."

The first person James saw as he boarded the train was Hywel, waving to him to him from the centre of the carriage. They sat together, talking of 'old times' until the train stopped at Gateshead.

They arrived just in time for the opening ceremony. Soon after, they came upon their mates. Rick and Gus were talking to their former colour sergeant, (who was by now, lieutenant colonel).

A strange young quartermaster kitted them out with new uniforms.

"You must return these uniforms, when your part in the proceedings is over." He ordered.

Eleven actors were also kitted out in the same uniforms, and another group of actors were given the apparel of Zulu warriors. They were to perform the re-enactment of the battle.

An official showed James and his comrades to their seats in the front row. He informed them that when the theatrical performance was over, they were to be introduced as the brave soldiers and survivors, of the actual battle of Rorke's Drift. The V.C. recipient was to lead the small procession on to the rostrum.

Lastly, the lieutenant colonel would be called upon to say a few words. After which they would bow to the audience and march back to their seats.

James was impressed with construction of the set, which was a replica of the cordoned off, south section, of the former mission station.

During the performance, which lasted for more the half an hour, James found himself having difficulty breathing. The fake ammunition used in the rifles let off clouds of smoke. This was causing him and his comrades, in the front row, to cough and sneeze profusely. In point of fact, they were glad when it was all over, so that they could make their way to the refreshments tent.

"Well now, this is a nice surprise." Gus exclaimed, as they walked into the tent. "I was not expecting free beer, were you, boys?"

Rick laughed. "This suits me all right, mate. I can't wait to get the taste of that bloody smog out of my mouth."

Hywel and a few of the other old soldiers had joined James, Gus and Rick. "This is just the job then, boys. Good health to you all." Said Hywel, raising his glass and grinning widely.

Having spent several happy hours with his good friends and comrades, James decided it was time to call it a day. More than half of the old soldiers had left already.

"Right, Hywel, mate, we should drag ourselves away. If we are to get the last train home, we should get a move on."

"I can't believe how fast the day has gone," Rick exclaimed, "so it's goodbye once again, boys, 'til the next time. I am hoping there will be a next time; we had better make it soon though, because, my friends, I fear we are all in God's waiting room."

"I for one am not going to leave on that note," Gus said with a grin, "only the good die young, and we are living proof that we don't come in to that category. So let's hope that we will all be around for a few more years yet."

"Here! Here!" was the joint reply.

Hands were shaken, goodbyes were said, and the old comrades went their separate ways. Each of them wondering, who, if anyone, would be missing the next time.

James, arriving home late in the evening, went straight to his bed. Although he was very tired, he was unable to sleep. Moving quietly, he rose, went into the kitchen, where he made a hot drink, which he took to his room.

Eventually, he fell into a deep sleep. He dreamed of his beautiful Emma — they were walking, hand in hand, along Swansea beach. Suddenly, she let go of his hand, she ran ahead, laughing, then she turned and beckoned to him. He was disturbed by a strange noise and then a knocking sound in the distance.

"Gramps, it's me, Edna, can I come in?"

James felt weird, he couldn't find his voice! 'What is wrong with my face?'

When he tried to speak, he could hear himself making weird noises.

Edna was standing over him. She looked so much like his Emma, that for a moment, he thought she was his lovely wife.

"Oh, my God!" she exclaimed. "Gramps, can you hear me?"

He managed to nod. He was strangely aware of what was happening to him. He was dying, Emma was calling to him, and he was happy to go to her.

EPILOGUE

James Owen was buried with full Military honours, aged eight-seven.

Along with his numerous family, many friends, and members of the press, those also mourning his passing were: Lieutenant Colonel Bourne, the remaining survivors of Rorke's Drift, a contingent of the South Wales Borderers, in uniform, together with buglers.

The abundant wreaths and floral tributes from family and friends also included: large poppy wreaths from your comrades in arms, the remaining survivors of Rorke's Drift, the South Wales Borderers, the old comrades association, the caretaker and staff of Brecon Museum, the British Legion.

James' medal was given by his family to Brecon Museum.